YULE LOGS AND MURDER

A CHOCOLATE CENTERED COZY MYSTERY

CINDY BELL

CONTENTS

"I will never, ever, get tired of the smell of this place." Ally Sweet took a deep breath of the air laced with the scents of chocolate, cake, and various sweet flavors. "It still takes me back years whenever I walk in here. I will always treasure spending so much time here as I was growing up."

"That's lovely to hear." Charlotte Sweet looked up from the Yule log she had just finished frosting. "I told you I would take care of the shop. I thought you were going to take a couple of hours off?"

"I had planned to, but Luke got called into work, and I wanted to spend some time with you, so I thought I'd stop by to help out. I want to try and get on top of the Christmas orders." Ally smiled as she stepped up to the table beside her grandmother. Her fiancé Detective Luke Elm seemed to be constantly busy at the moment. "I hope you don't mind the interruption."

"Not at all. I have to say, sometimes I miss not working here as much as I used to, but I think mostly, I miss working with you." Charlotte met Ally's eyes. "We've had some good times here, haven't we?"

"The best." Ally sighed as she closed her eyes for a moment. "And some of the hardest."

"So true." Charlotte wrapped her arms around her in a tight hug. "But we made it through them all, didn't we?"

"Yes, we did." Ally smiled. She turned to open a cabinet above one of the counters.

"No, don't look in there!" Charlotte pushed the cabinet closed.

"What? Why? I was just looking for some of the candy canes that you said you were going to crush over the top of the cake." Ally narrowed her eyes.

"Just leave that cabinet alone. I've been working on some ideas for the wedding." Charlotte grinned and rubbed her hands together. "I can't wait!"

"Oh, the wedding." Ally feigned a heavy sigh and rolled her eyes. "I'm so tired of talking about that."

"Not a chance." Charlotte burst into laughter. "I

know you're more excited than I am, if that's possible."

"I am." Ally chewed on her bottom lip. "I just hope that Luke is."

"Why would you think he isn't?" Charlotte frowned as she brushed her hand along Ally's back. "Are you two having some trouble?"

"No, no trouble at all. It's just that he's always so busy, and when I try to talk to him about the wedding, it kind of feels like I'm bothering him." Ally shook her head. "It's probably just me being a little over sensitive."

"It could be. But you should talk to him about it. Communication is so important." Charlotte grabbed the crushed candy canes from another cabinet. "Do you want to help decorate?" She offered the bag to her.

"Sure, I'm happy to help." Ally took them. "Especially if I get a taste! Is that your whipped ganache frosting?" Her mouth watered as she headed straight for the Yule log, eager to get a taste of the homemade chocolate frosting.

"Oh no, hands off!" Charlotte gave Ally's hand a light swat before her fingertips could dig into the log. "This is for the common room at Freely Lakes, not for you."

"Aw!" Ally frowned as she drew her hand back. "But it smells so good!"

"I know, which is why the other one only lasted a few hours. When I left there were only a few slices left over. Hopefully, this one will last a little longer." Charlotte laughed as she waved Ally away again. "There are a couple to choose from in the shop."

"I know, but they're not as good as this one, this one was made by you." Ally sprinkled the crushed candy canes over the cake.

"You made the other ones." Charlotte shook her head as she began to pile the utensils and bowls into the deep sink.

"Exactly, that's the problem." Ally nudged her lightly to the side with her hip and took over washing the dishes. "No matter how many times you show me how to do it, it just doesn't taste the same when I make it."

"Your Yule logs are delicious." Charlotte laughed as she wrapped up the log. "But I promise, I'll make another one for you tomorrow."

"Thank you." Ally grinned. "How are things at Freely Lakes anyway? Are things still going missing? I know that Luke said he's heard about a few more reports in the last week of stolen items."

"Yes, things are still being taken." Charlotte

frowned. "I think the police believe that we are just forgetful and lost the items. No one is breaking in and just a few things go missing. The police aren't taking it too seriously I don't think, but the manager has promised us that he will find out what's happening. We think it might be an inside job, otherwise how else can they get access to our apartments without breaking in. Unless they are just highly skilled and covering their tracks. Luckily, I haven't had anything taken."

"Mee-Maw, do you want to come stay with me until all this is settled?" Ally turned toward her. "It can be like old times. You, me, Peaches, and Arnold all under one roof again." She looked into her eyes.

"Ally, that's a very sweet offer. But I want to stay at Freely Lakes. I have to find out who's behind this, and put an end to it." Charlotte raised her eyebrows.

"I'm sure you'll have it figured out in no time." Ally turned back to the dishes.

"I hope so." Charlotte sighed. "Some people are really angry about it. Ricco had his late grandfather's watch stolen right out of his dresser drawer. He has no idea when, but when he went to look for it, it was gone. He is furious about it, and he threatened the manager that if he doesn't do something about it, he will be facing a lawsuit. I'm not sure if he has any ground to stand on, but I wouldn't blame him if he tried." She frowned. "Enough talk about this stuff, though. I want to talk about the most important part of the wedding."

"The kiss?" Ally grinned.

"The cake!" Charlotte laughed.

"I don't care, as long as it's chocolate." Ally licked her lips. "Will you make it?"

"Of course!" Charlotte slipped the Yule log into a box and sealed it up. "I'm not sure that Luke would go for chocolate, though. Maybe he wants something else."

"I'm not sure that he cares either way. Anyway, who doesn't like chocolate. I know he does." Ally rinsed soap suds from her hands. "Let me take that out to the car for you."

"It's alright, Ally, I can get it." Charlotte picked up the box. "I'll leave you to clean up, though. I want to get this back to Freely Lakes before people start roaming the halls in search of more."

"And they will, it's just that good." Ally opened the back door that led into the courtyard specifically designed for Arnold and Peaches to enjoy, with a pig pen for Arnold. "But I thought you might have two minutes to say hello to Arnold and Peaches before you leave."

"Oh absolutely. I didn't know they were here." Charlotte handed Ally the box and crouched down to greet Arnold. The pot-bellied pig squealed and ran over to Charlotte. "Hi buddy." She let him nuzzle her hands. "So good to see you." She smiled as the orange cat pranced over to her and rubbed against her leg. "Hi Peaches." She stroked her back. "I have to get back to Freely Lakes, but I'll come visit again soon." She kissed Arnold on the head, but Peaches was already walking toward the other side of the courtyard and had stopped to sniff a flower. "Lost interest already." Charlotte laughed.

Ally gave her grandmother back the cake box and held open the gate that led from the courtyard out into the parking lot for her.

"I might have to come by Freely Lakes later and snag a piece."

"You'd better hurry, because it won't last long." Charlotte waved to her as she headed through the gate.

Ally closed the gate behind her, then returned inside to the sink to finish the dishes. As she piled them on the dish drainer to dry, her thoughts wandered back to Luke. There was no question in her mind that he wanted to get married, but she did wonder if he looked forward to it as much as she did.

"Being a police detective is not an easy job, Ally," she muttered to herself and shook her head. "You're imagining things."

Ally turned her focus to the front door as a few customers stepped inside. When she had finished serving them, she concentrated on checking on the supply of boxed candies. The Christmas rush was in full swing, and it was hard to keep up with the demand sometimes. Although, there was a good amount, she decided to make some more, both to add to her supplies, and to calm her mind. Working in the chocolate shop her grandmother had handed down to her, always put her at ease.

❧

As Charlotte drove away from the chocolate shop, her mind settled on Ally for a moment and her comment about Luke not caring about the cake. She had made quite a few comments like that recently about Luke not caring about the wedding. Charlotte knew that even if he didn't care about the small details of the wedding, what he did care about was being married to Ally. From what she had seen he couldn't wait.

Sometimes Charlotte wished she could turn back time, to when Ally was just a child, and a warm hug and a fresh cup of homemade hot chocolate fixed everything. She recalled Ally's sweet childish laughter as it bounced off of the walls of the small cottage they had shared. She treasured that sound. Ally's laugh didn't sound quite the same now, but the light in her eyes, and the way she tossed her head back in glee, were identical. She wished her granddaughter all of the joy in the world, but she knew that life didn't always work like that. There would be ups and downs, but she trusted that Luke would be there through all of them. She hoped she hadn't misplaced her trust.

Charlotte turned onto the highway that led to the neighboring town of Freely, and her home, an apartment at Freely Lakes, a retirement community. Even though she was happy there, she felt a small tug in her heart to turn in the other direction, back to the small cottage that she had raised Ally in after her mother passed away. She could remember a time when she thought she would never be enough for her granddaughter, when she believed that the loss of Ally's mother at such a young age would stop Ally from ever having a happy life. Charlotte was relieved to discover that wasn't the case. Seeing Ally thrilled over her upcoming wedding, and head over heels in love with Luke, made her realize that things could always get better.

Charlotte believed that about Freely Lakes, too. Though there were some aspects of it that she found annoying, such as the pressure to join in on some social activities that she didn't enjoy, and the general cattiness of some of the ladies that lived there, there were other aspects that she absolutely enjoyed. Being surrounded by a community of the friends and familiar faces that she had spent most of her life around was a great comfort. And meeting new people had been great as well. She enjoyed sharing some treats from the chocolate shop with them.

Charlotte parked in Jeff's spot. Jeff had become a good friend of Charlotte's. He also lived at Freely Lakes and had lent her his car as he was visiting his grandchildren for the Holidays. She headed to the main entrance instead of her apartment. Inside of the large building were several multi-purpose rooms, including a common room that served as essentially a central living room for the residents to spend time together if they chose.

Charlotte had to admit that when she'd first

moved to Freely Lakes, she was eager to regain her independence, and give Ally the space she needed to blossom. She was eager to move on with the next stage of her life. But she had been hesitant about the place to a degree. She expected it to be all about shuffle board and bingo nights. Instead, the residents of Freely Lakes often engaged in activities that she found herself having a hard time keeping up with. Everything from bowling, to archery, to swimming competitions in the large indoor heated pool. It had grown on her faster than she expected.

Charlotte poked her head into the common room and felt a small sense of relief when she found it empty. Around Christmastime, she was the most popular person at Freely Lakes. Everyone wanted some of her chocolates. Even though Ally had taken over managing the shop, she was still Charlotte, of Charlotte's Chocolate Heaven, and she would always be the one they turned to for their sugar fix.

Having a few minutes to set up the Yule log without everyone crowding around gave Charlotte time to make it look nice. She added a few sprigs of pine from the large Christmas tree, around the base of the log. As she walked around the side of the table, closest to the fireplace, her foot knocked into something unexpected.

"Please, excuse me." Charlotte gasped, as she caught sight of the shoe she had kicked. The apology was instantaneous, before she had a chance to process the fact that no one should be lying on the floor of the common room. Her eyes traveled the length of the leg, as her heart pounded. Sprawled out beside the fireplace was a woman. Charlotte gasped, as she lurched toward her.

"Are you okay? Ma'am? Can you hear me?" Charlotte brushed the woman's long, dark hair away from her face, and instantly her heart sank. It was clear that she was not okay. In fact, she was dead!

CHAPTER 2

Charlotte's voice caught in her throat as she tried to call for help. While processing the shock of what she saw, a hint of recognition settled into the back of her mind.

"Nola," she whispered the woman's name as she struggled to get back to her feet. "Oh Nola, who did this to you?" As the words left her lips, she felt the strength in her voice return. "Help!" She shouted toward the still open door of the common room. "Please! Someone! I need some help in here!"

Charlotte turned back toward Nola, and nearly tripped over a thick log abandoned beside her body. She did her best not to think about how it was used to kill her. Had someone surprised her from behind? Did she even know what happened?

"Oh Nola, you poor thing." Charlotte clasped her hand over her mouth as a tremor carried through her entire body.

"Charlotte?" Kevin, one of the staff members, poked his head into the common room. His tall and broad frame filled the doorway. "What's wrong? What do you need help with?"

"Kevin, you must call the police." Charlotte's heart raced as she realized the commotion she'd made had drawn the attention of other people in the hall. "Don't let anyone else in here! This is a crime scene!"

"Huh?" Kevin stepped farther into the room. "Has there been another theft?"

"No, it's not a theft. There's been a murder!" Charlotte gestured to Nola's body, half-hidden by the table beside the fireplace. "Please, just make sure no one gets inside."

"Oh no!" Kevin gulped as he stared at the body.

Charlotte noticed how pale his skin became, and the way his muscles tensed. "Kevin, snap out of it, please, I need your help." She walked over to the door as a few residents of Freely Lakes wandered inside.

"The common room is closed right now." She shooed them back out the door, then closed it.

As Charlotte turned back toward the fireplace, she saw that Kevin had finally put his phone to his ear. She heard him stumble over a description of what he saw. She couldn't blame him for struggling. How would she even begin to describe it if she had to?

Charlotte felt for her phone in her pocket and pulled it out. With a trembling hand she typed a message to Ally. She didn't want to frighten her, but she also didn't want her to hear about it first from someone else. She needed to make sure that her granddaughter knew that she was okay. Once she'd sent the message, she slipped her phone back into her pocket and listened to the comforting sound of the sirens in the distance.

They would be too late to save Nola, but at least the police could ensure the safety of all of the residents and guests at Freely Lakes. Her heart skipped a beat as she thought of the murderer, who had likely been in the common room shortly before she arrived. Who had done this to Nola? Was it a resident? Someone she passed in the halls each day? The thought left her unsettled, and a little dizzy.

"Charlotte." Kevin walked toward her, his blue eyes sharp. "Who did this? Did you see the person that did this?"

"No." Charlotte shook her head as her mind continued to spin. "No, I just found her like this." She squeezed her eyes shut, then took a deep breath. "There was no one else here."

~

"Peaches, what are you doing in the herbs again?" Ally shooed the orange cat away from the herb garden in the corner of the courtyard and sighed. "I know that you're curious, but you're not a gardener." She ran her hand across the cat's soft fur. "Why don't you keep Arnold company while I get this next batch of candies ready?" She gave her thigh a light slap, and the pot-bellied pig lumbered up to her. He snorted at her hand then chased after the cat.

Peaches bolted as if she was terrified, but the truth was she loved it when Arnold chased her. They could play together for an hour or so chasing each other before Peaches lost interest.

Ally had just stepped back into the shop when her phone beeped, alerting her to a new text message. She checked the message to find that it was from her grandmother. The words she read made her heart race.

Part of her hoped that it was an autocorrect mistake, but she knew better. Her grandmother would never make a mistake like that. She started to dial her grandmother's number, but before she could finish, the door to the shop swung open, and Luke stepped inside.

"Ally, I just heard about something that happened at Freely Lakes. We need to get down there right away."

"It's true?" Ally shoved her phone into her pocket and grabbed her keys and purse from behind the counter. "Mee-Maw just texted me, but I was hoping I didn't understand it right."

"I'm afraid it is." Luke held the door open for her.

Ally paused long enough to turn the open sign to closed and lock the door, then she followed him to his police car. "Do you think she's safe there?"

"I'm sure she is." Luke started the car, then glanced over at her. "There hasn't been any further reports of violence. My guess is, it was a personal confrontation. But I still want to get there as soon as possible."

"It's not your jurisdiction." Ally buckled her seat belt as he drove off in the direction of Freely.

"No, but I'm sure that they won't mind an extra hand in the investigation. We help each other out on occasion." Luke turned onto the highway. "I just hope that Charlotte is okay."

"Me too." Ally frowned as she looked down at her phone. "She's not answering. She might not be ready to talk, yet. Can you go any faster?"

"Yes, I can."

The car sped up far beyond the speed limit. Luke turned on the flashing lights on the top of his car, then the siren.

Ally knew that he didn't do either thing lightly. She guessed that he might be just as worried as she was.

Ally didn't feel any sense of relief until she stepped into the common room at Freely Lakes, and saw Charlotte with her own eyes.

She looked pale, but otherwise unharmed.

"Mee-Maw, are you okay?" Ally bolted toward her as her heart raced. "We came as soon as we heard!"

"I'm fine." Charlotte waved her hand in front of her face and took a deep breath. "I just didn't know what to do when I found her, Ally. I have no idea what happened."

"It's alright, Charlotte, we're going to find out." Luke rubbed his hand lightly across her shoulder, then stepped past her in the direction of the body.

"Mee-Maw, here, sit down." Ally pulled a chair over for her grandmother. "Are you sure you're alright?"

"I'm fine, don't fuss over me." Charlotte frowned as she waved her away. "It's not me that we should be worried about, it's this poor woman. Nola, I think her name was." She covered her mouth with one hand as she took a sharp breath. "Ricco's daughter-in-law. He was so excited about her coming to see him! Someone has to tell him." She started to stand up from her chair.

"We will." Ally guided her back down with firm pressure on her shoulders. "But you need to sit a moment, Mee-Maw, and get your breath."

"You're right." Charlotte drew a long, slow breath, then sighed. "I guess I am a little shaken up."

"Of course you are." Ally sat down in a chair beside her and squeezed her hand. "This is quite a shock." She swallowed hard, then looked into her eyes. "I can't imagine what might have happened if you interrupted the murderer."

"Don't." Charlotte shook her head. "No one else was here when I came in. I put out the cake. I even spruced it up a bit." She sighed. "I had no idea Nola was even here until I almost tripped over her."

"That must have been such a shock." Ally looked

over at Luke who had begun to speak with one of the Freely police officers. "Have the police spoken to you yet?"

"Not yet." Charlotte frowned. "They got here right before you did. They just blocked off the area." She pointed to the now taped-off area at the far end of the common room, by the fireplace. "I guess they are trying to assess the situation first before they speak to me. It's for the best. I have nothing to tell them." She spread her hands out in front of her. "I didn't see anything, I didn't hear anything. I keep going over it in my mind, looking for some clue that will tell me exactly what happened here, but Ally, I just wasn't paying any attention. I was focused on the cake, and nothing else."

"I'm sorry, Mee-Maw. I know this must be overwhelming for you." Ally ran her hand along her grandmother's shoulders. "Once the police speak with you, we can get you out of here."

"But who could have done this, Ally?" Charlotte frowned as she looked at her. "Who could have done this?"

"That's what we're going to find out." A man in a suit stepped up to Charlotte, his eyes narrowed. "I'm Detective Barrio. You're the one who found the body?"

"Nola, yes." Charlotte held tightly to Ally's hand.

"You knew her then?" The detective made a note on his phone.

"Yes, I knew her. Not well, but I had met her before." Charlotte filled him in on Nola's relationship to Ricco. "He's going to be devastated when he finds out. Someone should tell him, before the rumors spread."

"I'll take care of that." Detective Barrio nodded. "Here's my card." The detective held it out to Charlotte. "An officer will take your statement and I'll be in touch. Sometimes, as the shock wears off, details can come to the surface that you might have overlooked. If you think of anything at all, please contact me right away."

"Of course, I will." Charlotte tucked the card into her purse.

"Is that all you need from her, Detective?" Ally frowned. "I'd like to get her somewhere quieter."

"Yes, that's all I need for now." The detective looked between the two, then glanced over at Luke. "I'm sure you'll be kept up to date with what's happening in the investigation, but it may take some time before we make progress. At this moment, everyone in Freely Lakes is a suspect."

Ally watched as he strode back over to the body, then she looked at her grandmother.

"I'm just going to see if Luke has any information. You should stay here." Ally stood up and walked over to Luke. She noticed that Luke had the cleaner, Kevin, pulled aside. She knew him well as he had a sweet tooth and was a regular at the chocolate shop.

Droplets of sweat had formed on Kevin's forehead, and his thin, blue uniform shirt displayed a ring of sweat around his neck and chest. His red hair was wet and sticking to his forehead.

"I need to know who was in here in the last hour or so." Luke looked straight into Kevin's eyes. "Every person, don't leave anyone out."

"Do I have to say?" Kevin frowned as he glanced from Luke, to the area where the body had been found.

"It's best that you do." Luke took a step closer to him and narrowed his eyes. "Why wouldn't you want to?"

"It's just, everyone here is like family to me." Kevin clenched his hands at his sides, then frowned. "I guess, I just don't want to believe it could have been him."

"Who?" Luke's voice hardened.

Ally stood up and watched as Kevin squirmed under Luke's scrutiny.

"Kevin." Luke continued to hold his gaze. "I'm here to get to the truth. Someone was murdered, whoever did this, could hurt someone else. You need to tell me who you saw, so this person is caught and no one else is put at risk."

Kevin let out a small gasp, then nodded. "I only saw one person." He hesitated once more, then shook his head. "Ricco. I saw Ricco. I heard some arguing, so I wanted to see if everything was okay. When I looked in the room, it was Ricco and Nola. Everyone knows Ricco is a hothead, he likes to yell, but he doesn't cause any harm. I asked Nola if everything was okay, she insisted it was. So, I walked away." He looked down at his feet as he sighed. "Maybe I should have said something more than that. Maybe I should have done something."

"Did you see Ricco leave?" Luke crossed the small space left between them as Kevin continued to keep his head down. "Kevin, I really need your help here."

"Yes." Kevin sighed as he glanced up, then took a deliberate step back. "Yes, I saw him leave. But I don't think he saw me. He slipped out through the back door." His voice raised as he spoke again. "But he didn't do this, alright? Please, you have to believe me. Ricco's a good man, he would never hurt Nola."

Luke jotted a few notes down, then looked back into Kevin's eyes. "You did the right thing by telling me, Kevin. I promise you, I will conduct a thorough investigation into what happened here."

"Things like this aren't supposed to happen here." Kevin shook his head as he turned and walked away.

Luke looked up from his notepad and right into Ally's eyes.

"Is Charlotte alright?"

"She seems to be." Ally glanced over at her grandmother, then looked back at him.

"I spoke with Detective Barrio and he has a few officers off because of the Holidays, so he is happy to have my help on the investigation." Luke frowned as he looked down at his notepad. "Although, I'm not sure there will need to be much of an investigation. This Ricco person appears to be our best suspect. He knew the victim, was seen arguing with her shortly before she was killed, and leaving the room not long before her body was found." He glanced around the room. "It sounds pretty open and shut to me."

"Maybe." Ally glanced over at her grandmother who still sat on the chair. "But I don't think it's going to be that simple. Mee-Maw doesn't think Ricco would have done this."

"We never think people we know or care about are capable of murder." Luke tucked his notepad into his back pocket. "But unfortunately, they can be. I have a lot more evidence to gather, but so far, he's my main focus."

"If he did this, then he probably took off." Ally crossed her arms. "He's probably trying to get as far away as possible."

"Detective Barrio had his officers surround the property, so if he is still around, he isn't getting out of here." Luke tipped his head toward the door. "And it looks like the rumors are already flying."

Ally settled her gaze on a trio of women who each gave the police officers who stopped them from entering the room, hard stares.

Mrs. Bing, Mrs. White, and Mrs. Cale, always managed to be wherever the action was. Normally, that meant sidling up to the counter at Charlotte's Chocolate Heaven, for coffee and candies each day. But they had probably been in early that morning and now the shop was closed. They had probably headed straight for Freely Lakes the moment they sensed something was off.

"Young man, you're not listening to me." Mrs.

White narrowed her eyes. "I know my rights, and I know that you can't deny me entry to this room without just cause."

"Ma'am, I need you to step back." The officer did his best to sound polite.

Ally sensed his patience was wearing thin.

"I'll go speak to them." Ally stepped away from Luke and over to the officers gathered by the door. "Ladies, let's talk in the hall, and let these fine officers do their jobs. Okay?" She smiled as she herded them through the door and out into the hallway.

"Ally, is Charlotte okay?" Mrs. Bing gasped. "We heard that she's the one who found the body."

"Heard from who?" Ally frowned. "How did you find out?"

"Oh, everyone knows." Mrs. Cale laughed nervously. "There are no secrets around here."

"She's doing okay, thanks for your concern." Ally frowned. The three women had been part of her life as she grew up, like three honorary grandmothers who always wanted to know everything that was happening in her life. "What are the three of you doing here?"

"Oh um." Mrs. Bing licked her lips. "We'd heard that Charlotte was going to put out another of her chocolate Christmas cakes, and we just happened to have some friends we needed to visit here today, so we thought we'd pop in for a bite."

"I see." Ally held back a smile. The three were not shy about their affection for candy, especially those created at Charlotte's Chocolate Heaven. "Unfortunately right now, the common room has to stay off-limits."

"Such a tragedy." Mrs. White clucked her tongue.

"And during the Christmas season." Mrs. Bing huffed. "Bad things aren't supposed to happen around Christmas."

"Bad things happen all of the time. It doesn't matter what season it is, or what day it is." Mrs. White crossed her arms. "Statistically, this was bound to happen."

"Statistics, who is talking about statistics?" Mrs. Bing rolled her eyes. "The point is, it's extra sad this time of year, to lose someone."

"It is." Mrs. Cale pursed her lips. "Especially someone so young. What was she, in her forties?"

"Maybe even younger." Mrs. Bing clucked her tongue.

Ally walked them down to the end of the hall. "But that's why it's so important to let the officers conduct their investigation. You can help by making sure they don't have any more interruptions. Keep people away from the common room. Can you do that?" She looked between each of them.

"Yes, of course." Mrs. White gave a firm nod. "We will keep everyone away."

"Great, thank you." Ally felt some relief that they would remain occupied with their task.

As Ally started to turn away, a thought surfaced. She turned back to face them. "Have any of you seen Ricco around?"

"Ricco?" Mrs. Cale looked down the hallway. "Do you mean that Ricco?"

Ally turned just in time to see Ricco walk up to the door of the common room.

"We should stop him before he bothers the officers." Mrs. Bing started to walk toward him.

"No." Ally held up her hand to stop her. "No, I think the officers will be happy to speak with him."

Ally hurried back to the common room, eager to see if the murder would be solved right away. But would the killer really return to the scene of the crime?

CHAPTER 3

After calling Jeff to tell him what had happened so he didn't have to hear it through the grapevine and worry, and convincing him she was fine, Charlotte stood up. She noticed that Barnaby, the maintenance man for Freely Lakes, hovered just outside the door of the common room. From the troubled look in his eyes she guessed that he had just been informed of the tragedy. She started to wave to him, but an officer led him away before she had the chance to. She still had some trouble forming clear thoughts, but she was determined to work her way out of the shock that finding Nola had left her in. Just as she started toward Luke, Ricco burst through the door of the common room.

"What's happening in here?" Ricco stared at the

officers, then his eyes settled on the gurney with the body bag on it. "Who is that?"

Luke's shoulders straightened as he turned to face Ricco.

Charlotte's heart pounded as she realized that Ricco was about to be arrested for the murder of his daughter-in-law. She couldn't blame Luke. There was no reason to believe that anything else had happened. Yet, as she gazed at Ricco's frail frame she couldn't help but see him as an elderly man that needed her help.

"Ricco, you should sit down." She offered him the same chair that Ally had guided her to.

"Sit down?" Ricco shook his head. "I don't need to sit down. I just want to know what's going on here. The manager said we should all stay in our apartments. I was on my way back to mine, when I saw all of the commotion."

"Ricco Pace?" Luke walked up to him, his expression stern and his voice even.

"Yes, that's my name." A wide smile spread across Ricco's lips. "Why do you want to know?"

"I'm Detective Luke Elm." He showed him his badge. "One of the members of staff told me that your daughter-in-law, Nola, was visiting with you in here earlier." He raised an eyebrow. "Is that true?"

"Ah, yes. Well, my ex-daughter-in-law, actually. But she's such a sweetheart, she comes to check on me all the time." Ricco patted his rounded stomach. "Tries to keep me healthy. Why? What is this all about?"

"I'm sorry to tell you this, but Nola has been killed." Luke's voice softened, and his hand caught Ricco's elbow as the older man's knees threatened to buckle.

"No!" Ricco leaned into Luke's grasp. "No, that can't be true!"

"It is, Ricco." Charlotte cradled his other elbow with both of her hands. "I'm so sorry, but it is. Please, sit down."

Ricco slumped down into the chair and stared into space.

"Nola? You're sure it was Nola?"

"I saw her myself, Ricco." Charlotte ran her hand the length of his arm and hoped that the warmth of her touch would soothe him in some way. "I am the one that found her."

"It's just not possible." Ricco rocked forward and buried his face in his hands. "I just saw her, I just spoke to her, it couldn't have been more than an hour ago."

"I know this is a lot to take in." Charlotte looked

up at Luke as he cleared his throat. "Maybe you could tell us about that last conversation you had with her. Did she mention being worried, or scared?"

"We argued," Ricco muttered as he lifted his face from his hands. "Oh, how terrible is that!"

"Argued?" Luke stepped a little closer. "What did you two argue about?"

"She caught me." Ricco rubbed his hands along his cheeks as tears filled his eyes. "She caught me in the act."

"The act of what?" Charlotte felt her chest tighten. What could Ricco have been involved in that would drive him to kill Nola, after she found out?

"Your Yule log, Charlotte." Ricco wiped at his eyes. "It was just too delicious for me to resist. I promised Nola that I would only have one slice. She warned me it wasn't good for me, she wanted me to watch my diet, especially because I haven't been feeling so well lately. But I wasn't satisfied with one slice. I waited until I thought Nola left, then I came back. I just wanted one more slice. But she caught me." He took a sharp breath. "I told her, she had to stop treating me like a child, that I am a grown man, and I can eat what I want. And she got upset, she said that I needed to be more realistic about my health risks, and that she had put in a lot of time and energy to help me get better. I was embarrassed, and mad." He sighed. "I told her she had to stay out of my way, and out of my life, that she wasn't even my real family." He winced. "How could I say something like that to her? How could those be the last words she heard from me?"

"I'm sure she knew that you were just upset." Charlotte wrapped her arm around his shoulders and squeezed them. "I'm sure she didn't take them to heart."

"Is that all you argued about?" Luke's eyes remained fixed on Ricco. "You didn't have any other disagreements?"

"What?" Ricco stared at him, then shook his head. "No. Not at all. She only ever wanted to take care of me." He pulled his phone from his pocket. "I have to call Ronaldo. He has to know what happened. He's going to be heartbroken."

"Ronaldo, your son?" Charlotte patted his back. "Maybe you should give it a few minutes, let yourself calm down a little first."

"Ricco, I need to know where you just came from." Luke tried to draw his attention away from his phone. "Where did you go after you argued with Nola?"

"What? Why?" Ricco put his phone to his ear as he stared at Luke.

Ally walked up to the three of them. She looked nervously from Luke, to Ricco, then took her grandmother's hand.

"It's important that we find out everything we can about the last moments of Nola's life, so we can figure out who did this to her." Luke's eyes narrowed as his voice hardened.

"You think it was me?" Ricco's hand trembled as he gripped the phone. "Ronaldo! You have to get here fast. Nola's been killed, and the police think I did it!"

"That's not what I'm saying." Luke frowned as he nodded toward the phone. "Why don't you hang that up, please, so we can have a clearer discussion."

"No, Ronaldo says I shouldn't say a word to you." Ricco ended the call. "I have nothing else to say."

"Ricco, please consider that the person who did this to Nola, could be off harming someone else right now. Any information you give me, might help prevent that." Luke crouched down until he was face to face with Ricco. "Do you really want her murderer to go free? Is that what Ronaldo wants?"

"Not another word!" A man shouted from the doorway of the common room.

Charlotte gasped as she recognized his face.

"It's Ronaldo!" She tightened her grip on Ally's hand.

"Ronaldo!" Ricco bolted up out of his chair. He swayed for a moment, then grabbed onto Luke to steady himself. "I'm sorry, I get so dizzy when I stand up too fast."

"Sit back down." Luke eased him back into the chair. "Take a few deep breaths. I'll get someone here to look you over."

"No." Ricco's eyes narrowed. "No, I'm fine. I just need my son." He looked up at Ronaldo as he was allowed into the room. "Ronaldo, I'm so sorry. I don't know what happened. But Nola is gone!"

"My father is not going to speak to anyone without a lawyer present." Ronaldo stepped up beside his father. His thick, and muscular frame, as well as his towering height, made Ricco look tiny in comparison. "You have no right to be questioning him."

"We were just having a conversation." Luke took a slight step back and gazed at Ronaldo. "Did you just happen to be here? Your father didn't seem to be aware that you were so close by."

Ally's heart raced as she felt the tension crackle between Luke and Ronaldo. The other officers, as well as Detective Barrio began to gather around the two.

"I was just coming to see him." Ronaldo stood even taller. If he felt the slightest intimidation by the presence of the officers, he didn't show it. "Is that a crime now? To visit your father?"

"Ronaldo, they're just trying to help." Ricco reached for his son's hand. "Please, don't make this any worse than it is."

"What my father is not understanding right now, is that you are not here to help him. You are here to accuse him, and every single word he says is going to be twisted and used against him. If you think I'm going to stand aside and allow that to happen, you're wrong." Ronaldo placed his hand on his father's shoulder. "We are leaving."

"All we're trying to do is find out what happened to Nola." Luke stepped in front of Ronaldo before he could lead his father toward the door. "I'm sure you would want to know what happened to her."

"I know you suspect me of doing this. I don't buy your friendly attitude for a second." Ronaldo frowned.

"You can't think he had anything to do with this!" Ricco gasped.

"He's just trying to get information out of you,

Dad, and me. He obviously suspects us." Ronaldo flashed an icy smile at Luke. "You can poke around all you want. Nola and I had no problems. I was grateful that she took such an interest in my father's well-being. My father and I both loved her, she was still family to us. Maybe you don't understand what taking vows actually means, Detective, but I do. Even though our marriage ended, my responsibility to her, did not. The only thing I have to feel guilty about, is the fact that I wasn't here to protect her from the person that did this. Now, if you're through harassing my innocent father and myself, we'll be on our way. You have no right to hold us."

Luke frowned as he stepped aside. Ally sensed that it was taking all of his strength of will to do so.

The other officers stepped aside as well.

Detective Barrio walked with the pair toward the door.

"If you really mean what you say, Ronaldo, then you'll be willing to cooperate with us." The detective handed Ronaldo a card. "I'll need to speak to you in depth about any enemies that Nola might have had, and any interactions that might have concerned you. You and your father may be our best sources of information to find out what happened here. Please, don't let our desire to get justice for Nola offend you."

"I've got your card." Ronaldo tucked it into his pocket. "I'll call you when our lawyer can be at our side. Until then, you're going to have to do your job and find the actual murderer."

Ronaldo shook his head as he led his father out of the common room.

The moment the door closed, Detective Barrio turned back to face Luke.

"I can't begin to tell you how poorly that went." He frowned. "Our two best suspects are on the defensive, and they are not likely to tell us anything else that will help."

"Ronaldo is very defensive, isn't he. It looks like he has something to hide." Luke crossed his arms as he looked back at the other detective. "No matter what Ronaldo says, I am pretty certain that he wasn't too happy with Nola still being involved in his father's life. Why else would he have just shown up at the same time Nola was here, out of the blue? My guess is that he came here to confront her about interfering in his father's life. The only question is, was that before or after she was killed?"

"It's a place to start." Detective Barrio nodded, then turned and walked out of the common room.

Ally guided Charlotte out of the common room as well, leaving Luke to help with the questioning of anyone who had been nearby at the time of the murder.

"What do you think about what Ronaldo said?" Charlotte wrapped her arm around Ally's. "Do you think he meant it? That there were no issues between him and Nola?"

"I'd like to think it. But after being divorced, I doubt it. Things change when you divorce." Ally frowned as her heart fluttered. "But it's hard for me to imagine ever not wanting Luke to be part of my life, even if we didn't stay together."

"You don't need to imagine it."

"I know." Ally nodded. "Let's go back to your apartment for some coffee and to regroup, alright?"

"Yes, that sounds nice." Charlotte smiled.

"I'm sorry, Mee-Maw, I know this is a lot to handle." Ally placed a light kiss on her cheek. "But this is all going to get figured out. You need to rest."

"Ally, you know I love you, but I will not rest." Charlotte pulled away and looked into her granddaughter's eyes. "I am perfectly capable. I am not fragile."

"Mee-Maw." Ally frowned as she looked back at

her. "The world won't stop spinning if you let someone take care of you for once."

"Oh yes, actually, I think it will. This isn't the first dead body I've found and this isn't the first murder at Freely Lakes. You know I can handle it." Charlotte narrowed her eyes. "Now, are we going to figure out who murdered Nola, or are we going to stand around waiting for the dust to settle and the murderer to get away?"

"Mee-Maw, coffee first, then we can get started on finding out the truth." Ally steered her toward her apartment.

"No, I have a better idea." Charlotte pulled her phone out of her pocket. "If we want to find out some information about someone, I know exactly who to call. We can't get much further in our investigation, without knowing more about the victim. I doubt that Ricco or Ronaldo are going to be interested in talking to us." She placed the phone to her ear. "Luckily, we have someone who can help us find out all the dirt."

"What? Who?" Ally frowned.

CHAPTER 4

"Hi there, Christian." Charlotte sweetened her voice. "Any chance you're out at Freely Lakes?"

"Of course he is." Ally smiled as she shook her head. As a reporter eager to get his name in the paper, Christian always showed up anywhere a story might be.

"Great, why don't we meet you at the shop? I'll put some coffee on for us. The rumors are true, I was the one who found her." Charlotte paused, then winked at Ally and turned around in the other direction. "Sure, see you in thirty minutes." She ended the call and tucked her phone away. "See, simple as that."

"With Christian it's never simple." Ally followed after her grandmother.

"Maybe not, but he has quite a nose for the fine details, and I'm certain he can get us the information we need. He's already been here, but he is on his way back to Blue River for something, so we are going to meet at the shop." Charlotte continued toward the parking lot.

"Great, at least I can open the shop again." Ally smiled. "We'll have to take Jeff's car. Luke gave me a lift."

Ally followed after her as she headed toward the parking lot.

"You drive." Charlotte handed Ally the keys then got in the passenger side.

"Great." Ally got inside and started the car. "Christian's going to want information from you, too, Mee-Maw."

Ally was determined to keep up with her grandmother's plans.

"And I'm prepared to give it to him." Charlotte looked through the windshield as Ally turned onto the highway. "I know what happened at Freely Lakes today was tragic, but I can't get stuck in my shock, not when there is a woman who lost her life, and a murderer is out there. I need to do something."

Ally's heart softened as she pulled into the parking lot of the chocolate shop. Her grandmother's strength and determination had kept them both going through the years.

Charlotte glanced over at Ally, and wondered if she believed her. Had she done enough to convince her granddaughter that she was just fine? The truth was, she was a little rattled. She'd been rattled many times in her life, but she'd promised herself that she'd never let Ally see that. She wanted to be a rock for her granddaughter and if that meant hiding things from her now and then, that was what she would have to do.

When they reached the front door of the shop, there were a few handwritten orders taped to the door. Ally shook her head as she pulled them off and smiled. Christmas was always a busy time, but this year it seemed extra busy. Maybe it was because of the mild weather. They stepped inside and she dropped the orders by the register.

"I'll get the coffee started." Charlotte walked behind the counter.

"I'll get the cream and sugar out." Ally set up the counter with everything they would need.

Charlotte noticed that Ally seemed just as determined to be strong. She couldn't help but smile at the sight of it. When Ally had first moved back home after her marriage came to a screeching halt, with only her cat Peaches and a trunk load of possessions, she had wondered for a moment if she would recover, after facing so much loss in her life. But she had, and more than that, she had blossomed. She had opened her heart to a new relationship, an unexpected but happy one. She was far stronger than she looked, but she knew that her heart was huge and tender, despite her best efforts to shield it.

"I'm just going to check on Arnold and Peaches." Ally grabbed the few trays of candy from the display case that needed refilling and walked into the kitchen. The area of the large space where they made the candy had a large window that faced the front of the shop, giving customers the chance to see the process in action.

Ally placed the trays down, then she continued through the back door into the courtyard. While Arnold remained contained inside the courtyard, Peaches was becoming more adept at escaping, roaming the neighborhood to beg for treats from the neighbors.

However, as soon as Ally stepped outside, both pets bolted toward her, eager for their food, and some attention. She gave them some of both as she soaked in their affection.

"Alright, I know I took off on you today. Sorry about that." Ally smiled as Peaches nuzzled her cheek.

"I had to see them." Charlotte came through the back door behind Ally. "Hi babies." Both pets came over to nuzzle Charlotte's hand and immediately she felt more relaxed.

"I better go back inside to see if Christian is here." Ally stood up. "I won't be long." She smiled at Arnold and Peaches.

Ally walked back inside with her grandmother close behind her. Ally started to refill the sample trays and Charlotte tidied up the chocolate boxes on the shelves.

"Do you want to see if Luke is back in the area? You can let him know we are open." Charlotte turned toward Ally. "I'm sure he could use a cup of coffee."

"He'll be fine." Ally waved her hand. "I think he prefers I keep my distance while he's working."

Before Charlotte could respond, the bell above the door rang out.

Charlotte looked up to see a familiar young man come through the door. At times his nosiness left her exasperated, but at the moment she hoped it would lead her to exactly what she needed to know.

"Come in, the coffee's just about ready."

"Just finished." Ally called out from behind the counter.

Christian walked toward the counter.

"The coffee smells great, but I know I'm not here for chit chat." He stood by the counter.

"You're right. You're here about Nola, what can you tell me about her?" Charlotte grabbed the coffee pot and began to fill the mugs.

"I came here to ask you questions." Christian smiled at her and leaned against the counter. "So, what do I get if I answer yours?"

"I'll tell you anything you want to know." Charlotte set the coffee pot back on the burner, a hint of annoyance in her voice. "Don't hold out on us, Christian, I want to know what happened to this woman."

"Alright." Christian straightened up, nodded at Ally, then cleared his throat. "I'm sorry, Charlotte, I didn't mean to belittle what you went through."

"It isn't me that's dead, now is it?" Charlotte shook her head, then looked into his eyes. "What can you tell us about Nola, Christian?"

"Have some chocolate." Ally gestured to the

sample tray.

"I haven't had much time to dig." Christian popped a dark chocolate into his mouth and pulled his phone from his pocket. He ran his fingertip across the screen as he chewed. "From what I have gathered so far, it seems she was once a fairly well-known ballroom dancer. That's why I'm really going to look into the murder. I think this could turn out to be a pretty big piece." He looked up at her. "And of course, I want to find out what happened to her, too."

"A ballroom dancer?" Ally shrugged. "Luke and I are taking some lessons to get ready for the first dance at the wedding, it seems to be a popular thing for couples to do, and it's a bit of fun, but I didn't know that it was a thing someone could be famous for."

"It is, if you're a competitive dancer, and she was. Though, only briefly. She made quite a splash while she was on stage." Christian displayed a picture on his phone of a much younger Nola on a dance floor.

"I've seen pictures like that in the salon in town. One of the hairdressers, the owner actually, used to be a dancer, too, I think." Charlotte pursed her lips. "Though, I'm not sure if she was a professional."

"Really? What's her name?" Christian turned his

phone back to face him, prepared to take notes.

"Janene. She's very popular at Freely Lakes. She goes out there for a few hours a week and does the residents' hair in the salon there. Some of the residents can't or don't want to go into town." Charlotte watched as his fingers flew across his phone. "What else can you tell me about Nola?"

"She didn't have much family at the time." Christian lowered his voice, then met her eyes as he spoke. "She also wasn't named Nola at the time."

"What?" Ally set down the cup of coffee she'd been just about to take a sip from. "What do you mean?"

"She went by a different name. Ana. Same last name. I'm not sure yet if Nola is a middle name, or if it might have been a stage name or maybe Ana was, or why she might have changed it. I only discovered these pictures of her because I traced Nola back to an apartment which also had a tenant living in it previously by the same last name. Ana. I thought maybe Ana was a family member and she was the only one I had found, so I started looking into her and that's when I came across these pictures. Unless they are identical twins, Ana is Nola." A wide smile spread across Christian's lips. "Quite a scoop, huh?"

"It is, if it's true." Ally narrowed her eyes. "Isn't it

possible you've mixed up two people, somehow?"

"I guess we might find out when the police run her prints. I've already tipped off Luke to the possibility, so he's going to make sure that it's checked out. Anything to get on his good side." Christian winked at Ally. "Maybe then I'll be invited to the wedding."

"Oh stop it, you know you're already invited." Ally grinned at the mention of the wedding.

"Now, it's your turn." Christian turned his attention back to Charlotte. "I've told you what I know, I'd like to hear what you know."

"What do you want to know from me?" Charlotte shrugged. "Unfortunately, I showed up too late to stop the murder, or catch the killer."

"Any suspects?" Christian looked between them. "I know Luke's all over this. Just give me a hint. Anyone suspected right off the bat?"

Ally glanced over at her grandmother.

"None." Charlotte's hands tightened at her sides. She didn't want to cast suspicion on Ricco, she believed he was innocent. "None so far. At least, not that we know of. But I'm sure he will get to the bottom of all of this."

"Of course." Christian nodded. "And did you know Nola, Charlotte?"

"Only in passing. Ricco was always so eager to talk about her. Even after she and Ricco's son divorced, he still adored her. I saw them together on a few occasions, but I'd never really spoken to her." Charlotte sighed as she picked up her cup of coffee. "Now, I do wish I'd taken the time to get to know her better."

"So, the times you've seen her with Ricco, or heard him talk about her, he's never had anything bad to say about her?" Christian raised an eyebrow.

"He mentioned that she did get after him about his health. She seemed to care very much about his well-being. She always had him on some new diet or herbal remedy." Charlotte shook her head. "But other than that, I think Ricco was just pleased to have her attention."

"It's interesting that Nola was so attentive to Ricco, even though she and Ronaldo split up. Doesn't that strike you as odd?" Christian looked at the sample tray and picked up a mocha cream.

"Maybe a little." Charlotte glanced over at Ally. "But maybe she just had a good heart. Which makes this situation even more tragic."

"Indeed, it does." Christian smiled as he tapped on his phone. "Can I quote you on that?"

"Not a chance." Charlotte shook her head.

"I didn't think so." Christian winked at her, then gulped down the rest of his coffee. "Thanks for the brew and the chocolates. I've got to keep moving on this. I'll update you if I come across anything interesting, and I trust you'll do the same for me?"

"Of course." Charlotte smiled at him. "Thanks for the information, Christian."

Christian paused halfway to the door and turned back to face her.

"Take care of yourself, Charlotte. Whoever did this is still on the loose."

"Thanks. I'll keep that in mind." Charlotte nodded.

As Christian opened the door a customer came in to pick up an order. After they had left, Ally went to the kitchen to find her grandmother melting some chocolate.

"You don't have to do that, Mee-Maw." Ally smiled.

"I want to. It helps me relax." Charlotte continued stirring. "Why don't you get the Christmas-themed molds the kids love so much and we can discuss what we know."

"Perfect. Do you think Nola was running from something?" Ally got the molds from a cabinet above the sink and placed them in front of her grandmother. "Maybe that's why she changed her name?"

"Could be. Or it could be that she just didn't like her name anymore." Charlotte shook her head as she considered the options. "If she was as well-known as Christian described, then perhaps she didn't want people to recognize her as the dancer she used to be. Maybe she just wanted a fresh start and the easiest way for her to do that was to change her name."

"I can understand that." Ally began melting some white chocolate for her gingerbread truffles. "There was a time in my life that I wished I could be someone else, just for a little while."

"I think it's pretty safe to assume that Nola's early years weren't happy ones, if she decided to leave them behind." Charlotte began pouring the milk chocolate into the molds. "The problem is, we don't know anyone who can fill us in a little more on that. If she did change her name to leave the past behind, maybe someone from the past found her. Maybe that person tracked her down, right here to Freely Lakes, and decided to settle some kind of score."

"It's definitely possible." Ally set the melted chocolate aside to cool slightly and got the prepared gingerbread balls out of the refrigerator. "Although, Ricco's argument with her, and Ronaldo being nearby when the murder took place, are both pretty damning possibilities, too."

"You're right. They both had the opportunity." Charlotte began cleaning up. "Ronaldo's claim that there were no issues between the two of them sticks out in my mind. I think I'm overdue for a trip to the hair salon." She ran her fingers through her hair. "What do you think, Ally?"

"I think your hair looks great, as always." Ally raised an eyebrow. "But I'm guessing this visit isn't for the haircut as much as it is for the information?"

"Yes. Maybe Janene knows Nola because they were both into ballroom dancing. And, everyone gossips at the salon. I'm sure if there is anything to know about Ronaldo and Nola, I will find out about it there. I'll give her a call and see if she has an opening." Charlotte began to scroll through the numbers on her phone.

"I'll go with you." Ally collected the dirty utensils and placed them in the sink.

"You'll do no such thing. It'll seem strange to show up with you at my side. Besides, I am sure that Peaches and Arnold need some attention and you have work to do. I promise, I'll report back anything I find out." Charlotte smiled as she looked up from her phone. "Janene has an opening."

"Alright, but please be careful, Mee-Maw. Christian is right, as long as the killer is on the loose, you need to keep yourself safe." Ally frowned as she stepped away from the sink.

"As I always do." Charlotte gave Ally a quick hug. "Please, don't worry about me. There's so much to be excited about right now, with the wedding plans."

"You know I'm always going to worry." Ally met her eyes. "The wedding doesn't matter right now."

"Of course it does, honey." Charlotte cupped Ally's cheeks. "Make sure you spend some time with Luke whether he likes it or not. He needs you, too, you know."

Charlotte grabbed a small box of chocolates and walked through the back door. She was tempted to turn back. She wanted to tell Ally to seize the joy in the moment, and not let anything weigh her down, that life was too short to dwell on the darker parts. But she knew it would be a waste of time. Being young had its downfalls, not the least of which was worrying about everything and everyone. Once she had achieved a certain age, she had learned to relax and let go. But Ally still had quite some time before she would reach that mindset.

Charlotte said goodbye to Arnold and Peaches and headed to her car.

CHAPTER 5

As Charlotte neared the salon, she prepared herself for what she might find out. Although she did enjoy Janene as a stylist and she was a customer at the chocolate shop, she didn't know too much about her personally. She recalled the pictures on her wall of her ballroom dancing. Was it really possible that she would know of Nola, or Ana, as she was once called?

"Charlotte, come in." Janene smiled as she gestured to an empty chair in front of a large mirror. "I'm not scheduling any other appointments right now. I thought you might prefer the privacy."

"Thanks Janene. I brought you these, nut clusters. I know you like them." Charlotte handed her the box.

"Thank you." Janene smiled as she took the box.

"I guess you've heard?" Charlotte sighed as she sat down in the chair.

"Yes, yes I have. I was at Freely Lakes this morning." Janene picked up a brush. "Just a trim?"

"Yes, please. Not too much." Charlotte settled back in the chair and smoothed down the cape that Janene draped over her.

"Just enough to freshen up the look." Janene smiled at Charlotte through the mirror as she began to brush through Charlotte's long, gray hair.

"Janene, I've noticed your pictures on the wall." Charlotte pointed to one of the framed photographs. "You were in ballroom dancing competitions?"

"Yes." Janene smiled some as she smoothed down a few strands of Charlotte's hair. "It feels like a lifetime ago. I used to think I would never stop dancing."

"Why did you?" Charlotte continued to study the photograph.

"The choice was taken from me." Janene set the brush down hard in the tray beside her. "That's how life goes sometimes. I was doing quite well in the competition, so well that my career would have been launched. My partner, Matthias, was one of the fiercest and most talented competitors. His determination pushed me hard, and I danced better than I ever thought possible."

"That sounds like an experience that would transform you." Charlotte settled back in her chair as she felt Janene's fingers pull through her hair.

"It was. Until, she showed up." Janene rolled her eyes in the mirror, then picked the brush back up. "Over all these years, never once did I believe that our paths would cross again. In fact, I didn't recognize her. She came in here with Ricco when he wanted a trim. I had no idea who she was. But I did notice that she looked at all of my pictures, then left in a hurry."

"Nola?" Charlotte feigned ignorance as she heard the scissors snip through her hair. "Was she a dancer, too?"

"Oh yes. She was a dancer. A good one, I have to admit. She could have been great, but she wasn't disciplined enough. She was always skipping practices and showing up late for competitions. Her partner bailed on her because of it. But she didn't lose easily. Instead of bowing out, she set her sights on Matthias, and manipulated him into becoming her partner. I was the one left without anyone to dance with, and she and Matthias won the competition." Janene sighed as she took a step back.

"It wasn't an easy time in my life, that's for sure. I thought I would never recover from the betrayal. But life goes on, doesn't it?"

"It does." Charlotte nodded as she gazed at her hair in the mirror. "It looks nice, Janene, thank you."

"You're welcome. Sorry about the trip down memory lane. Speaking to the police today has really stirred things up for me." Janene bit into her bottom lip as she met Charlotte's eyes in the mirror. "I wish I had known it was her. I would have had a few things to say to her."

"Like what?" Charlotte stared back into her eyes.

"It doesn't matter now, does it?" Janene shrugged as she picked up the broom to sweep up the hair she'd trimmed. "I'll never get to say any of it to her now."

"Sometimes it can still be therapeutic to talk about it, and just get the words out, even if the person you need to say them to isn't around anymore." Charlotte stood up and brushed off her blouse, though there weren't any stray hairs on it. "You're always ready to listen to anyone, I'm here if you want to get anything off your chest."

"Maybe it's best I didn't get the chance to speak to her. For so many years I've believed that everything happened as it was meant to, I had no other choice but to believe that. If I had told her how I felt about her stealing Matthias from me, and the win, and then wasting it, maybe she would have said something to make me feel sorry for her. I don't want to feel sorry for her. I'm sure there are those brokenhearted over her death, and I do feel sorry for them. But Ana? Or Nola, as she called herself? No, I don't think I will be shedding a single tear over her getting what she deserved." Janene winced, then glanced toward the still open door. "Of course, if anyone heard me say that, they'd probably think I'm the murderer."

"I wouldn't say that, Janene, we all have a right to our feelings." Charlotte gave her a light pat on the shoulder, then paid her for the haircut.

As Charlotte walked out of the salon, she wondered if Janene decided to use actions instead of words to let Nola know exactly how she felt.

～

After her grandmother had left to go to the salon, Ally went outside to check on Arnold and Peaches.

They ran over to nuzzle her hands.

"I just need to get some orders boxed up, then I'll

get you two home. Then I have to go out again, I'm afraid. But don't worry, I'll bring you home some treats."

Ally went back into the shop. She put on some Christmas music to help her relax and clear her mind, then she put on her gloves and began boxing up some Christmas-themed boxes, with different shaped and flavored chocolates. From Santa, to sleighs and reindeer.

The music, the scent of chocolate and the repetitive task immediately helped her unwind. There were quite a few customers picking up orders and from what she could tell, word about Nola's murder hadn't got around yet. She knew it would soon.

The shop was finally empty and Ally was about to go out the back when she heard the bell over the door jingle. She looked up to see a man who was both broad and tall. She recognized him immediately.

"Kevin?" Ally smiled. He was a chocolate lover and a regular at the chocolate shop. She knew that he worked at Freely Lakes and had been there when her grandmother had found Nola's body.

"Ally, I was hoping you would be open. I need

some chocolate." Kevin smiled sadly as he looked at her with puffy eyes.

"What can I get for you, Kevin?" Ally asked. "A box of your favorites and a hot chocolate?"

"Ooh, yes please." Kevin only smiled slightly but his eyes lit up.

"Peppermint or caramel?" Ally gestured for him to take a seat at the counter.

"Um, peppermint." Kevin shook his head. "No, caramel."

"Why don't I make you a peppermint one for now and a caramel one that you can make up at home?" Ally suggested.

"Perfect." Kevin smiled. "Thank you."

"How are you holding up?" Ally boxed up his favorites, milk chocolate hazelnuts and dark chocolate caramels, and put a couple on a small plate in front of him.

"I'm okay." Kevin frowned.

"It must have been quite a shock." Ally made a peppermint hot chocolate for him as well as one for herself. She placed them on the counter.

"Yum, smells delicious." Kevin sniffed the steam coming from the top of the mug. "I just can't believe this happened."

"Me either." Ally shook her head. "It must have been a shock."

"It was." Kevin nodded. "Luckily, your grandmother was there. She is so calm."

"She is." Ally smiled. Her grandmother always impressed her with her quiet confidence and composure.

"I hope I didn't get Ricco into trouble." Kevin shook his head. "He cared so much for Nola. He would never hurt her."

"You had to tell the police." Ally reassured him. "They'll work it all out."

"I don't know if I can go back to Freely lakes." Kevin looked into his cup as if looking for answers.

"Things will get easier. It's still a shock." Ally shook her head.

"No, it's not just this." Kevin took a sip of his drink. "It's just so tense there. Albert and Barnaby are always at each other's throats these days." He bit into a milk chocolate hazelnut.

"Albert and Barnaby?" Ally tried to meet his eyes. "Why?"

"Albert has never liked Barnaby. He blames him for the thefts, for not doing his job properly." Kevin frowned. "And now this happened."

"What do you think?" Ally took another sip as she listened closely.

"I don't think Barnaby could ever steal from the residents. He forgets to do things, but he is so nice to the residents." Kevin finished his hot chocolate, just as a couple came in to pick up their orders.

"Mary, Anton." Ally greeted them. "Your orders are ready." She put the boxes on the counter.

"Thanks Ally." Anton picked up the boxes and they left.

When they closed the door, Kevin stood up and pulled out his wallet.

"How much do I owe you, Ally?"

"Nothing, something to brighten a difficult day." Ally smiled as she handed him his chocolates.

"Thanks, Ally."

"Just take it easy." Ally smiled. "Things will get better."

"I already feel a lot better." Kevin turned and walked toward the door.

Ally checked the clock, then turned the open sign to closed and locked the door. As she finished off boxing up the chocolates, she ran through what Kevin had told her. Could the arguing between Barnaby and Albert have something to do with Nola's murder? She couldn't see how. Ally closed down the register and wiped down the counters, then walked out the back.

Peaches and Arnold ran up to her. She crouched down to give them a pet.

"Sorry, I took longer than I thought." Ally put on their leashes. "Let's get you home, babies."

Ally dropped off Peaches and Arnold at the cottage. She played with them for a bit. Their loving, happy, mischievous attitudes always brought a smile to her face and even made her forget about the murder for a few minutes.

Ally made sure they had everything they needed, then headed back to Freely Lakes. No matter what her grandmother said, or how capable she was, she didn't want her to be alone.

CHAPTER 6

When Ally got to Freely Lakes, she saw Luke's car there and remembered her grandmother's words about spending time with him. She decided to take her advice and try to catch up with him before she went to see her grandmother. She headed straight to the common room to find it sealed off with police tape, but empty of police officers. She headed from there, to the lobby. In the lobby she noticed a few patrolmen speaking to residents, but saw no sign of either detective working the case.

Ally guessed that Luke was already hunting down a lead. She slipped her phone out of her purse and considered texting him, but decided against it. He needed to focus, and her interrupting his investigation was not going to help things. Instead, she decided to have a look around the grounds of Freely Lakes for any signs of the murderer fleeing the scene. She walked around behind the building until she reached the windows of the common room. A small garden stretched from one end of the building to the other, directly beneath the windows.

The only person that Kevin had seen leave the common room was Ricco. If someone else had come and gone, maybe he had missed them, or maybe, they had chosen to exit the room a different way.

Ally walked the length of the garden in search of any crushed stems or footprints in the soft soil. The pristine blossoms had unblemished petals and the soil surrounding them appeared undisturbed.

"So, no one climbed out the window, at least from what I can tell," Ally muttered as she peered up at the building again. "Which means the killer had to both enter the room from inside, and leave the room from inside." She wondered how many ways there were to access the common room. There were two doors she had seen, but there was also a kitchen adjoining the common room. Could someone access the room through the kitchen?

Ally headed back toward the lobby in hopes of speaking to the manager. She stopped in her tracks when she heard whispering. She looked toward the sound of the voices. She noticed they were coming from behind a bush growing in front of a window of the manager's office. She thought she was imagining things and started to walk again, when she heard the noises again. Ally's heart raced. Was someone hiding in the bushes waiting to attack her?

Ally thought about forgetting about it but decided to investigate further. She decided she was just being paranoid. She stepped closer to the bush. As she did she heard someone say, "Shh," in a loud whisper.

Ally stepped closer and saw peeking out the side of the bushes, a very distinctive, red hat that she recognized.

"Mrs. Bing!" Ally stepped closer and peered around the back of the bush. Sitting down behind the bush were Mrs. Bing, Mrs. Cale and Mrs. White. Six eyes stared up at her. Their shoulders relaxed when they saw it was Ally.

"Lucky it's you, Ally. I told you to be quiet." Mrs. Bing swatted at Mrs. Cale's arm as she stood up.

"Can you help me please?" Mrs. White held out her hand to Ally, who grabbed it and helped her to her feet. When she stood up she brushed off the back of her dress.

"What are you doing?" Ally looked at the three women crowded around her.

"I um, I lost my earring." Mrs. Cale grabbed her ear which had a small, gold loop earring in it. "I was looking for it."

"It's in your ear, Mrs. Cale." Ally laughed.

"I know." Mrs. Cale smiled. "I just found it."

"I don't believe that for a second." Ally crossed her arms.

"Oh, all right." Mrs. Bing shook her head. "We just wanted to see if we could find out any information about what happened to Nola."

"We were looking around, seeing if we could find a clue, then we saw Detective Barrio speaking to Albert the manager, through the window." Mrs. Cale pointed to the window they had been in front of. "And we wanted to see if we could hear anything."

"And did you?" Ally tried to hide a smile. She loved the way the three women were always in the middle of everything, trying to help out.

"No, they were talking too softly, then you turned up. We tried to crouch down but our knees aren't what they used to be." Mrs. White brushed off her dress again.

"Speak for yourself." Mrs. Bing crossed her arms

and raised her chin slightly. "I managed to crouch down. I am very nimble. You made me sit down."

"That's because you kept standing up in between." Mrs. Cale huffed.

"Well, at least I was quiet." Mrs. Bing stared at Mrs. Cale. "Mrs. Cale almost got us caught."

"I did not." Mrs. Cale scowled.

"You did. You sneezed just as he walked up to the window." Mrs. White shook her head. "You are such a loud sneezer. You can't afford to be so noisy on a stakeout."

"Rubbish." Mrs. Cale huffed. "I am a dainty sneezer."

"Dainty?" Mrs. Bing laughed.

"Enough, ladies." Ally looked between the three women. They were the best of friends but they could certainly bicker with each other. "You really shouldn't be sneaking around, you should leave the investigating to the police."

"Oh, don't try that on us." Mrs. Bing crossed her arms. "If you and Charlotte get to investigate, then we do, too."

"But you need to be careful." Ally frowned.

"We are being." Just then Mrs. Bing's phone beeped. She looked at it and gasped. "Oh no, we have to get going." She started walking toward her car.

"Come ladies, it's time to drop off the presents at the hospital."

"Already? Where did the time go?" Mrs. White waved over her shoulder to Ally. "Keep us in the loop. We'll do the same."

"See you in the chocolate shop!" Mrs. Cale called out.

Ally smiled as she watched them. She hoped that she would have as much energy and such good friends at their age.

Ally continued to walk around the building toward the lobby, hoping to speak to the manager about how the common room could be accessed. Before she could get to the door, she spotted Luke alone in his car, not far from the entrance. With the door still open, he still had one foot on the ground, but his eyes were locked to his phone. As she started to approach, she received a text on her phone.

A quick glance at it revealed it was a message from Luke.

Just about to head back to the station, are you and Charlotte alright?

"We're okay." Ally smiled as she paused beside the car.

"Ally." Luke met her eyes as a smile spread across

his lips. "I saw your car and was hoping to catch you before I left."

"Here I am." Ally leaned against the side of the car. "How is the investigation going?"

"At the moment, neither of the prime suspects have an alibi, which should make this easy. The problem is, there's also no physical evidence so far to connect either of them to the crime. The lab will analyze the log from the fireplace, which we believe to be the murder weapon, and hopefully they will find something on there." Luke smiled up at her. "It will take some time, though. Right now, I'm trying to track down any connections that Nola, or Ana, might have had."

"Christian told us about the name change." Ally frowned. "Why do you think she changed it? Did you find any criminal history for her?"

"Not at all. That's the first thing I assumed. Maybe she got into trouble with the law and wanted to distance herself from her previous name. But I haven't come across anything that indicates that. It seems Ana grew up in Freely, but she disappeared when she left ballroom dancing professionally, and then I can't find any sign of her until she shows back up here a couple of years ago as Nola. She took off somewhere for sure, but wherever it was, I can't find any trace of her. Then something brought her back home." Luke sighed, then shook his head. "She had so little family. I keep getting caught up in the idea that I'm missing something, or someone. As it stands now, besides Ronaldo and Ricco, I can't find any other family for her."

"Hopefully, you'll find another relative." Ally smiled. "The only two people that we know were involved in her life, are the main suspects in her murder."

"I really thought this was going to be an open and shut case. But I'm starting to suspect that this is going to take more time to unravel." Luke stood, took her hand and pulled her gently toward him. "I'm sorry, I know how distracted I get when I have a case to solve. Please don't think I'm not looking forward to Christmas, or excited to plan the wedding."

"You don't have to apologize for being devoted to your job, Luke." Ally kissed him as his arms slid around her waist. "I'll do anything I can to help you."

"I know you will. But you leave the investigation to me." Luke looked into her eyes. "You have a lot on your plate right now, with Christmas sales at the shop, and dinner with Charlotte to plan, and the wedding to plan, and now with me tied up with the investigation. I'm sure things will get pretty chaotic. I just wanted to make sure I checked in and let you know how important you are to me."

"How did I get so lucky?" Ally grinned, then leaned forward for a quick kiss. "I love you, Luke."

"I love you, too." Luke squeezed her hand. "I should really get back to the station, I have a few leads to follow up on. There are some people she might have had connections with when she was still Ana."

"Good luck." Ally kissed his cheek.

"Thanks, I'm sure I'm going to need it." Luke closed his door and started the car.

Ally watched him drive away, then walked toward the door of the lobby. He was right, she did have a lot to juggle, but even without him by her side, just knowing that she had his love and support was enough to make her feel capable of handling it all.

CHAPTER 7

Moments after Charlotte arrived back at her apartment, she heard a light knock on the door.

"Ally, I've told you before, you don't need to knock." Charlotte rolled her eyes as she opened the door.

"How did you know it was me?" Ally's eyes widened as she looked at her. "How could you just open the door to some random person?"

"I didn't, I opened it to my granddaughter. Unless, you're not her?" Charlotte raised her eyebrows.

"Mee-Maw, you know what I mean." Ally frowned. "Especially at a time like this, you have to be more careful."

"Ally, I knew you wouldn't stay away very long. I estimated the amount of time it would take you to lock up and finish the orders in the shop and take care of Arnold and Peaches, and though I might have been off by about ten minutes, I figured that time was spent getting an update from Luke. Was I wrong?" Charlotte smiled as she grabbed her hand and pulled her inside of the apartment, then closed the door behind her.

"No, you weren't wrong." Ally sighed as she shook her head. "You are just amazing, as always."

"Good answer." Charlotte grinned as she led her into the kitchen.

Ally explained her conversation with Kevin and how she had caught the three ladies snooping around.

"Hopefully, they find out something without getting caught." Charlotte laughed. "I spoke to Janene, and she had a lot to say. In fact, she knew Nola when she was Ana." As she filled her in on the betrayal that Janene experienced, Ally settled at the kitchen table.

"Wow, that sounds like some bad blood between them. And she claims she had no idea who Nola was? I'm not sure if I believe that."

"It has been many years since they were dancing."

Charlotte frowned. "She didn't look the same as she did in those pictures that Christian showed us. Different hair color and style, she was much thinner years ago, and of course she's aged. And she changed her name. I think it's possible that she didn't recognize her."

"Luke's on the hunt to find any connections to Nola's past, before she changed her name, but so far he hasn't turned up anyone." Ally narrowed her eyes. "I guess Janene would be the only one who knew her back then, but she didn't know her well enough to offer any further insight. Do you think she might have done it?"

"She certainly has some motive to go after Nola." Charlotte sat down at the table with Ally. "But I'm not convinced that she is the one who did this. I would think that if she had been the one to kill Nola, she would want to hide her connection with her, not discuss it."

"That's a good point." Ally sat back in her chair. "But it's also possible that she knew that the police would find out about her connection either way. Maybe she thinks that it makes her look less guilty if she talks about it openly." She frowned. "Maybe she decided to confront Nola once and for all, and whatever Nola had to say angered her so much that she lost her temper and killed her. We know the murder weapon was right there at the scene. The police lab is analyzing it for any evidence that might indicate who wielded it. But the fact that it was just grabbed out of the pile of wood in the fireplace makes it seem as if this wasn't planned out beforehand. It seems more like a crime that happened in the heat of the moment, and the killer just grabbed whatever was available."

"I think so, too. Which does make it seem possible that Janene could have done it." Charlotte pursed her lips. "But it's such an old wound. Janene has a completely different life now. Could something that happened so long ago really stir up so much anger that Nola is dead because of it?"

"It's hard to say, without knowing exactly how much Janene wanted to be a successful dancer, or how much she has festered over what Nola did back then. A grudge can be a very powerful thing."

"That's true." Charlotte watched as a few residents walked past her kitchen window. They looked in the direction of her apartment and began to whisper. "I guess I'll be the talk of the neighborhood until something more interesting comes up."

"I still think you should come back home with

me. What if Ricco is the one who did this? He might come after you next. Or even his son. I just don't feel comfortable with you staying here." Ally frowned as she watched another group of residents join the first.

"Ally, you know I will be perfectly safe here. The police are going to be present until they get a good handle on what happened here. There's nothing to worry about." Charlotte patted the back of Ally's hand.

"That's what you said about the thefts." Ally shook her head. "First, things are going missing from apartments without any sign of forced entry, now someone has been murdered. I intend to speak to the manager about it. Make sure they're doing what they can to keep you safe."

"Actually, that's not a bad idea." Charlotte stood up. "We should talk to the manager. If he's been monitoring the thefts, as he claims he has been, then he might have some information about who was lingering around the common room today. Let's go see what we can find out." She led the way to the manager's office. She'd been there many times before. "I've spoken to Albert a few times about the thefts recently. He insisted that he was on top of it. We aren't exactly on the best of terms at the moment." She hesitated a few steps from the partially open door. "Maybe we should get our stories straight before we go in."

"Shh." Ally put her finger to her lips as she heard a sharp voice from behind the door.

"Barnaby, you will tell them that there was no issue between Nola and me, do you understand?" The manager's voice carried out through the door.

"So, you want me to lie to the police?" A younger, rougher voice, responded with just as much volume. "And what happens when they find out the truth? Do you think that is going to go well for me?"

"It's not a lie! We didn't have any problems between us!" Exasperation weighed down Albert's voice.

"I heard the two of you argue just this morning, because that light bulb hadn't been changed in Ricco's room." Barnaby's voice grew even louder. "She was furious!"

"It was just a stupid argument, one you caused by not changing the light bulb in the first place! I should have fired you on the spot for not doing your job, but I didn't, did I?" Albert took a deep breath. "We need to make sure we have each other's backs on this. That's all I'm saying. It won't matter to the police that the argument was over a silly matter, they will make a big deal out of it, and I can't have that."

"I don't know, Albert, I don't like it. I don't want to say anything to them at all!" Barnaby's voice faded into a whine. "I just want to go home for the day, and stay out of it."

"No way. I need you here. Already the residents are on my case about the thefts, and now this? I need every available employee here, making sure that we look fully staffed and capable. We could have a mass exodus after this, and then we'll all be out of a job. Is that what you want, Barnaby?" The scrape of chair legs against the floor carried through the door. "Tell me, is it?"

Charlotte gazed into Ally's eyes as they both listened for Barnaby's response.

"Alright Albert, I'll do whatever you say. Just try to keep my name out of it, will you? I don't need the police digging where they shouldn't."

The door began to swing open.

Ally gasped as she grabbed onto her grandmother's arm. She pulled her into the closet next to the manager's office, just before Barnaby walked out into the hallway.

"Well, that supports what Kevin told me, that Barnaby and Albert often argued. I doubt they wanted to be overheard," Ally whispered. She peeked around the edge of the door. "I think he's gone."

"I'd say Albert has a lot to hide." Charlotte peered around Ally's shoulder into the hallway. "It seems to me that we should be considering him a possible suspect."

"Really?" Ally frowned. "But what motive would he have?"

"I'm not sure, yet. But if he's that worried about hiding the argument from the police, then there's a reason. Maybe there is more to the argument than he's saying." Charlotte nodded toward the closed door. "Should we go have a conversation with him?"

"Not yet." Ally stepped out into the hallway. "I want to talk to Luke about it first. If he has the heads up, he might be able to dig a little deeper, and find out more information than we can about Albert."

"Good idea. But first, I'm going to speak to her." Charlotte pointed to a volunteer that walked toward them. "If there was something more going on between the two of them then Marge would know about it. She keeps tabs on the community around here." She waved to the woman as she stepped out into the hall. She had a huge heart and loved to gossip.

"Marge!"

"Charlotte, there you are." Marge frowned as she pulled her into a hug. "I've been so worried about you. How are you holding up?"

"I'm alright, thanks." Charlotte pulled away and looked into her eyes. "But I just can't believe that Nola is gone, and right here, under the roof we share."

"Yes, it's quite shocking." Marge shook her head, then smiled at Ally. "It's so good that you came here to check on your grandmother. I feel bad for Ricco, he won't have Nola coming to visit him anymore." She sighed.

"He still has Ronaldo, at least." Ally stepped out from behind her grandmother, her eyes lingered on the office door, which hadn't budged.

"Ronaldo?" Marge shook her head. "No way, before Nola he never visited. Ricco would tell me all about his wonderful son, but I never laid eyes on him until Nola brought him to see Ricco. After the divorce, he rarely ever came, but Nola still did."

"He was here today, though." Ally looked over at her. "Just in time to comfort his father."

"My guess is he wanted something." Marge rolled her eyes.

"You may be right about that." Charlotte glanced at the office, then lowered her voice. "We just heard a terrible argument between Albert and Barnaby. Are things okay between the two of them?"

"Things have been tense lately." Marge lowered her voice as well. "There are rumors that Albert suspects Barnaby is involved in the thefts that have been happening here."

"Really?" Charlotte gasped as she feigned ignorance. "I would never believe that. He's so kind and helpful."

"I agree. I think Albert is just in a panic and pointing fingers. That's why I advised Barnaby to record any interactions he has with Albert. I said it's always best to make sure you have yourself covered in case of any accusations. Hopefully, he's doing that. I suggested a phone app that I use whenever I feel like I need a little extra security. It's easy to turn on, and no one ever notices that it's happening. Instant Record. It records everything." Marge frowned. "But who knows if he listened to me. Most people don't."

"I hope he did." Ally's heart skipped a beat. If Barnaby had listened to Marge then there was a good chance that the argument between Albert and Nola had been recorded.

"Me too. I'd better get back to it." Marge smiled as she walked past them down the hall.

"Mee-Maw, do you think Albert is right about

Barnaby stealing from the residents here?" Ally had already started dialing Luke's number.

"I'm not sure. I've never suspected him." Charlotte frowned. "But I intend to find out."

"Hi Ally, how's Charlotte holding up?" Luke's warm voice drew her attention back to the phone.

"She's doing okay. But we just discovered something that might be very helpful to the investigation." Ally filled him in about what they had overheard, as well as the information that might be on Barnaby's phone.

"I've heard of that app. If he has recordings of any interaction between Albert and Nola, I'd love to listen to it. Unfortunately, unless he willingly hands over the recordings, I won't be able to listen to them."

"Why not?" Ally frowned as her hand tightened on the phone. "Luke, this could break the case wide open! Albert had an argument with Nola just hours before she was killed!"

"I hear you, Ally." Luke sighed. "But I can't force Barnaby to turn over his phone. Not without cause, or a warrant. So, until we can find out more about what's on it, or more about how Barnaby might be involved in the crime, there's nothing I can do about it."

"What about him possibly being involved with the thefts? Isn't that enough reason to confiscate his phone?" Ally's determination waned, she already knew the answer to her question.

"Not without some real proof that he's involved. Just some gossip isn't going to be enough. My guess is Albert will never admit to employing the person that is stealing from his residents. I doubt he'll file an official complaint, even if he has evidence that Barnaby is involved. We're stuck right now, Ally. But you gave me some great information to work with. I really appreciate it. I'll let you know what I turn up."

As Luke ended the call, Ally let out a heavy sigh.

"This is so frustrating! We know that Barnaby knows something, but we can't get to the truth. Sometimes I think Luke has to follow too many rules!"

"Those rules are in place for a reason." Charlotte gave Ally's shoulder a light pat. "But luckily, they don't apply to everyone."

"What do you mean?" Ally met her eyes.

"I mean, if someone were to accidentally pick up Barnaby's phone, thinking it was theirs, and scroll through it a bit, it's not even considered a crime. Right? It's just a person making a mistake. It certainly can't be considered a crime if the person isn't caught, either, right?"

"Oh Mee-Maw, you are always coming up with the best ideas." Ally shook her head as she grinned. "But how are we ever going to get our hands on Barnaby's phone? I doubt that he's going to give it to us."

"We'll just have to distract him and make sure that we search quickly. You'll have to be the one to look through the phone, because it takes me forever to navigate through those things." Charlotte rolled her eyes. "I see the advantage to them, I really do, but it's hard to keep up with all of the changes in how they work."

"I can do that, Mee-Maw, but he probably has a passcode on it. We have to be able to break through it." Ally bit into her bottom lip, then nodded. "Maybe if we can get him to open his phone, and then put it down, we could get into it. There's usually a short delay before the lock screen comes back on. That should give us enough time to get to what we need to know."

"Perfect, I have a plan." Charlotte smiled. "Follow me."

CHAPTER 8

As Charlotte stepped back into her apartment, she dialed Albert's number.

"What's the plan, Mee-Maw?" Ally followed her inside.

"Just a second." Charlotte closed the door, then took a breath as Albert answered. "Albert, dear, thanks so much for picking up. I know how busy you must be."

"It's no problem at all, Charlotte. What can I help you with?"

"Would you mind sending Barnaby to my place? I'm having some trouble with a leak under the sink. I know everything's crazy today, but I'm just worried that it's going to turn into a bigger problem if I don't have it fixed now."

"Of course, no problem. Anything that you need. I'll have him come over right away."

"Thanks so much, Albert." Charlotte ended the call and met Ally's eyes. "So, Barnaby will come to us. When he gets here, I'll get him to unlock his phone. Then you have to knock me down."

"What?" Ally stared at her grandmother. "I would never do that!"

"Ally please, enough! I can handle a little tumble. If you want to solve Nola's murder, then we need to get into Barnaby's phone. All you have to do is give me a little push, I'll do the rest. Once I hit the floor, Barnaby will be quick to help me. I know, I've seen him help many people around here. Hopefully, he'll put his phone down in the process, and you'll be able to snag it. I'll keep him busy tending to me for a few minutes. You'll have to be very quick."

"Since we know the name of the app, I should be able to find it pretty fast." Ally frowned. "But I don't want you to get hurt."

"Ally, haven't we talked about this?" Charlotte quirked an eyebrow.

"Yes, alright." Ally sighed. "But Mee-Maw, what if—"

A sharp knock at the door silenced Ally.

Charlotte's eyes widened. She hadn't expected

Barnaby to arrive so quickly. She gave Ally a thumbs up, then hurried to the door.

"Charlotte." Barnaby frowned as he stepped inside. "I'm so sorry about what happened this morning. Are you doing okay?"

"Yes, as okay as I can be. I hate to be a pest, but this leak under the sink should probably be fixed before it floods the whole place." Charlotte led him toward the kitchen. "Are you sure you have time to take a look?"

"Of course I do." Barnaby started to crouch down in front of the cabinet under the sink. "How long has it been leaking?"

"Oh, not too long." Charlotte caught his hand and pulled him into a standing position again. "Barnaby, can I be honest with you?"

"Of course you can." Barnaby glanced at Ally, then stared at Charlotte. "What's going on here?"

"It's just, after what happened this morning, I'm nervous." Charlotte bit into her bottom lip, then shook her head. "I just don't feel safe."

"I can understand that." Barnaby frowned. "Is there anything I can do to help?"

"The truth is, there's no leak under the sink. I just wanted to talk with you myself. I know that Albert does the best he can with security here, but I just don't think it's enough. I don't want to tell him that, that's why I asked for you to come over to look at the sink. So, I'd have a chance to talk with you."

"I see." Barnaby nodded as a faint smile crossed his lips. "Yes, I wouldn't count on Albert for much."

"You're always here. I see you helping residents all the time. You know us, and we know you." Charlotte squeezed the hand she still held. "I feel like I can trust you, Barnaby."

"You can." Barnaby's voice wavered as he shook his head. "I would never let anything happen to you, Charlotte, I hope you know that."

"I do." Charlotte smiled. "That's why I want to ask you for a big favor. It might be overstepping, and I'm sorry if it is."

"Anything you need, Charlotte, anything at all." Barnaby patted the back of her hand. "Just name it."

"Would you mind giving me your cell phone number? Just in case I need you to check on things for me?" Charlotte blushed as she glanced at her feet, then back up at him. "I know that it's a lot to ask."

"It's just fine." Barnaby smiled, then pulled his phone out of his pocket. "I'll put your name and number in my phone, too, that way if you call I'll know exactly who it is."

Charlotte pulled out her phone and typed in the

number he rattled off. Then she watched as he unlocked his phone, and opened a new contact window for her number. As she gave it to him, she gave Ally a slight nod.

"Barnaby, this is so kind of you." Ally stepped forward. "I've been so worried about leaving my grandmother here alone, but knowing she has someone to call makes me feel so much better." She moved closer to him, then caught her foot on the leg of the kitchen table. She gave a short cry as she stumbled forward and bumped right into Charlotte.

Charlotte felt the light push, and exaggerated its impact. She gasped as she pretended to trip over her own feet and landed on the floor right by Barnaby's feet.

As Ally hoped he would, he dropped his phone on the kitchen table and reached for Charlotte's hand.

"Are you alright? Are you hurt?"

"I'm so sorry, Mee-Maw!" Ally steadied herself on the kitchen table with one hand and snatched the phone up with her other hand.

"Oh, my hip." Charlotte moaned as she swatted away Barnaby's hand. "Oh, just give me a second, I can't get up just yet."

"We should call for help!" Barnaby turned to reach for his phone.

Before he could, Charlotte grabbed his hand and pulled it hard. "No! Don't do that! I'm fine really, I just need a second. Please, just stay with me for a minute. I'll be fine in a minute."

"Alright, I'm here." Barnaby crouched down and held her hand. "Are you sure you don't need an ambulance? What if you broke your hip?"

"It's not broken. It's already starting to feel better." Charlotte sighed. "I just need a second to get my head together."

"Mee-Maw, I didn't mean to. I'm so sorry, I just tripped." Ally had her back to both of them. "I can't believe I did something so stupid."

"It's okay, Ally." Charlotte continued to cling to Barnaby's hand. "I'm fine. Just a little surprised. Barnaby's here to help me up. Everything will be just fine."

"We really should try getting you on your feet." Barnaby frowned as he looked Charlotte over. "The sooner we find out if you're injured the better." He glanced over at the table. "Where did I put my phone? We should at least have the nurse come and check you out."

"Oh, it's okay." Charlotte tugged his hand hard

again. "I think I can get up now. Just help me, please?"

"Sure, of course." Barnaby guided her to her feet.

Charlotte dragged out the process. The moment she was upright, Ally bent down and reached under the table.

"Barnaby, here's your phone." Ally handed it to him. "It must have fallen under the table."

"Thanks Ally." Barnaby smiled slightly. "Don't worry, accidents happen. I'm sure your grandmother will be fine."

"He's right." Charlotte smiled. "I'm just fine." She raised one knee, and then the other, to prove it. "Fit as a fiddle. Nothing to worry about."

"That's a relief." Ally hugged her grandmother.

"Don't worry. I'll keep a close eye on Charlotte for you." Barnaby slid his phone into his pocket. "If you need anything at all, Charlotte, all you have to do is call. Anytime. Got it?"

"Got it." Charlotte smiled. "Thank you so much." She walked him to the door and gave him a small box of chocolates. "I feel so much better just knowing you'll be close by."

"Good. Thank you for these." Barnaby gestured to the box, gazed at her a moment longer, then nodded at Ally before he continued out the door.

Charlotte closed the door behind Barnaby.

"What did you find?" Charlotte turned to face Ally. "Anything?"

"I found something." Ally frowned as she walked over to her. "Are you sure that you're not hurt? You really looked like you might be for a second there."

"I missed my career in acting." Charlotte grinned, then patted Ally's arm. "I'm fine, I promise. But I'd like to know what you found. Was the app on his phone?"

"Actually, no. Unless he has a way of hiding it. I couldn't find it. But I did find something interesting." Ally held up her phone. "I took a picture of it, so we'd have some proof that it was on his phone."

"Is that Nola?" Charlotte's eyes widened as she stared at the picture of a picture on the screen. "It looks like he snapped a picture of her in the garden here at Freely Lakes without her knowing it?"

"Exactly." Ally narrowed her eyes as she looked at the picture again. "I think Barnaby may be more involved with Nola than we thought. It isn't normal for a man to take a photo of a woman without her knowing. He's either stalking her, or he had a reason to take that picture."

"Barnaby is always alone. I've never seen him

with a girlfriend. But of course, he wouldn't necessarily bring a girlfriend to work with him. He doesn't talk too much. Maybe he just keeps his private life private. But I certainly never noticed him and Nola spending any time together." Charlotte shrugged. "But then I didn't know Nola very well either."

"Whatever the reason, he has her picture. I saw the picture when I opened his messages. It looks like it was sent from his phone to someone yesterday, which means that it looks like he was quite interested in her as of yesterday. But why would he send someone a photo of Nola. Maybe he had a crush on her? That could put him in conflict with Ronaldo."

"If Ronaldo was still interested in Nola." Charlotte nodded. "Yes, that's very possible."

"Unfortunately, just finding the picture doesn't tell us too much." Ally sighed. "We can't exactly tell Luke about the picture, it's not like he will be able to do anything with it after the way we found it."

"Let's go see if we can find out anything else from the residents." Charlotte headed for the door.

"I just wish we had more of a lead on what happened here." Ally started down the hallway in the direction of the common room.

"I think we're getting closer." Charlotte sighed. "It was disappointing that Barnaby didn't have the app or recordings on his phone, but now at least we know that he took a picture of Nola shortly before she died. Maybe he saw more than he's saying. Maybe he knows more than he's saying."

"Maybe." Ally walked into the lobby and spotted Luke near the door to the common room with Ricco and Ronaldo standing right beside him. Albert hovered at a small distance from the three.

Ronaldo's voice was already raised as he spoke.

"No one is going to tell me what I can or can't do!"

"I'm not trying to tell you what to do, Ronaldo." Luke's tone remained calm, but his posture stiffened. "I'm just reminding you that both you and your father need to remain in the area in case there are further questions that need to be answered."

"He's not staying here tonight. I won't allow my father to continue to live in a place like this. Not only has he been stolen from, but now someone who was like family to him has been murdered. Is there no security at all around here?" Ronaldo shook his head. "It's not safe. He'll be coming home with me tonight, and I won't hear any arguing about it."

"That might be for the best." Ricco stepped closer to his son. "I don't feel safe staying here tonight."

"I understand your concern." Albert glanced from him, to Luke, then back again. "We are doing our very best to ensure the safety of all of our residents. Obviously, we can't prevent everything. But we will increase the presence of security guards."

"And those cameras that are broken?" Luke stepped toward him.

"Yes, of course. I'll make sure they are fixed by tomorrow morning." Albert winced. "The funds are not always available to make the improvements that are needed, so sometimes some things get sacrificed in the interest of others."

"And that's how Nola ended up dead, with no idea who did it?" Ronaldo glared at him. "Now, my father has to face the scrutiny of the police because of your negligence."

"As I said, I will work hard to remedy the situation." Albert's voice tightened.

"Good for you, but that will do nothing to bring back Nola. What's done is done, and until I know for certain that this place is safe, my father will not be back here." Ronaldo took his father's arm. "Let's go, Dad, we aren't supposed to be speaking to any of these people without our lawyer." He shot Luke a stern look. "If you have further questions, you can contact him."

Ronaldo and Ricco brushed right past Ally and Charlotte and walked through the door.

"That didn't go well." Luke looked at Albert.

"Excuse me, I need to speak to Barnaby about the cameras." Albert gave a quick nod to Charlotte and Ally, then headed toward the stairs.

"How are you, Luke?" Ally looked into his eyes.

"I'm okay." Luke smiled. "I just hope those two don't decide to take off before we can gather enough evidence against them."

"With you on the case, I'm sure you'll get the evidence." Charlotte smiled as she met his eyes. "I feel so much better knowing that you're working on this with Detective Barrio. Speaking of him, where is he?" She glanced around the empty common room.

"I'm not sure. I've been keeping him up to date on everything I discover but he hasn't been in contact with me much. I'm sure he's following up on a lead, though." Luke smiled. "I'm going to go to the station, now." He gave Charlotte a quick hug and Ally a quick kiss, then left the room.

Charlotte stood in the middle of the common room and took a deep breath.

"It's only been a few hours, but it feels more like

days. I had hoped the killer would be found quickly." She looked over at Ally. "I think we should take the rest of the evening to relax and regroup for a fresh start tomorrow. There's not much more we can do today."

"You're absolutely right, Mee-Maw, Peaches and Arnold are probably wondering where I am." Ally frowned as she stopped herself from suggesting that her grandmother come home with her. She'd made it clear that she didn't want Ally being overprotective.

"Great. If you think of anything just call me, and I'll do the same for you. When we have clear, well-rested minds in the morning, I'm sure we'll come up with a lead to follow."

"Let me walk you back to your apartment." Ally started toward the door.

"Oh, I can find my way." Charlotte smiled. "Just go on home, Ally, before Peaches breaks out and starts looking for you."

Ally laughed at the thought of her cat roaming all the way to Freely to find her. Peaches had become a masterful escape artist recently and had been known to hunt Ally down all over town.

"Oh, that reminds me." Charlotte stopped walking and turned toward her. "I got a Christmas present for Peaches."

"You did?" Ally smiled.

"Well, it's more for you. It's a tracking device. A little box you attach to her collar, so if she goes wandering and you can't find her, you can track her on your phone."

"That sounds great, Mee-Maw."

"I thought it might be helpful." Charlotte shrugged. "Although, I have no idea how to set it up."

"I'm sure we can work it out."

"I'll be in early tomorrow to help you." Charlotte smiled.

"Don't worry about that, you rest, I can handle the orders." Ally shook her head.

"I know you can, but I want to help." Charlotte nodded. "You better get home to Peaches and Arnold."

Ally smiled, her grandmother was right. Maybe she could handle the orders. But one thing she wasn't so great at handling, was a hungry pig, and a hungry cat.

"Okay, Mee-Maw." Ally hugged her, then looked into her eyes. "See you tomorrow."

CHAPTER 9

The moment Ally left Freely Lakes, Charlotte snapped into action. She'd formulated the plan when she heard Ronaldo insist on taking his father home for the night. So far she'd been able to find a bit of information about Nola, and a bit about Ronaldo, but she wanted to see if she could find out more about them.

When Nola came to Freely Lakes, it was to spend time with Ricco. Charlotte had been inside Ricco's apartment before and she had seen many pictures of Nola and Ronaldo inside, even though she hadn't looked closely at them. Maybe the pictures might hold more information about Ronaldo and Nola and maybe even Nola's past as Ana. She had hoped that Ricco would let her have a look at them, but since he would be gone for the night with his son, she would have to see if she could get a peek inside his apartment herself.

Charlotte's heart pounded as she headed in the direction of Ricco's apartment. She knew that Ally would be furious with her for leaving her out of the clandestine adventure, but she couldn't risk her granddaughter being caught breaking into someone's apartment. Especially not when she was about to marry a police detective. She guessed that the wedding wouldn't go too smoothly if the bride showed up in handcuffs. She hovered near Ricco's door and glanced around to be sure that the hallway was empty.

Charlotte looked up and down the hall. Not seeing anyone, she tried the handle on Ricco's door. It turned just a little, then stopped. Locked. Of course, it couldn't be that simple.

With Charlotte's heart in her throat, she wondered if she could pick the lock with something she had in her purse. She fished through the contents in search of something that she could attempt to use. Of course, she had no idea how she would use it once she found it. As she dug a little deeper, a Christmas tree beside Ricco's door caught her attention. It was beautiful and green, with a few

Christmas decorations on it. Tucked beside the tree was a small watering can. It didn't take much inspection to recognize that the tree was fake, and would never need to be watered. So, why was there a watering can? Just for decoration?

On a hunch Charlotte picked up the can. A light jostle revealed the sound of something sliding around inside. A key? She guessed that Ricco might have left a key available for Nola to use, or maybe she had left it there in case he lost his own key, as Ricco could be forgetful at times. It seemed risky considering things were being stolen from residents' apartments, but maybe he forgot it was there. Charlotte plucked the key from the watering can and set the can back down where she had found it.

As Charlotte slid the key into the lock, she glanced around again. If anyone saw her, they might assume that she was the one who had been stealing from the residents. Of course that was a ridiculous idea, but she still didn't want to be caught. She tried to turn the key, but it wouldn't budge. She jostled it again and it didn't work. She sighed and dropped the key back into the watering can.

Just as Charlotte was about to search through her purse for something else to use to open the door, she heard a sound down the hallway. She looked down it, in the direction of the sound to find it completely empty. Was someone watching her? Waiting to catch her? She stepped away from the door just in time to see John, a local resident, walk around the corner. As he got closer, she could see that he carried a box of Christmas decorations.

"Charlotte." He grimaced. "So sorry to hear that you found Nola's body."

Charlotte sighed with relief that she hadn't been caught. She liked John's direct approach, he always got straight to the point.

"I know, it's terrible. I feel so sorry for Nola."

"Me too." John nodded, then lowered his voice. "Especially seeing as she was going to be set up for life. Ricco was going to leave her half his money."

"What?" Charlotte's eyes widened.

"I shouldn't say anything but he changed his will only last month." John said proudly, as if he held a secret. "He got me to witness the documents. His lawyer was here in the common room with him when I walked in and he asked me to witness them. He changed his will to leave Nola most of his money. He changed it from Ronaldo getting it all to Nola getting more than him."

"He did?" Charlotte's eyes widened.

"Yes, and between you and me he is actually a

very wealthy man. I saw it for myself. I know that he used to own a lot of property in the area that he sold off before he moved here." John patted the box in his hands. "Anyway, I have to decorate the Christmas tree. I will catch up with you soon."

"Yes, see you soon."

John continued down the hallway.

Charlotte ran over in her mind what she had just learnt. What would spark Ricco to make changes to his will? How would Ronaldo feel about the changes, if he found out? Did it have anything to do with Nola's murder?

Charlotte thought about trying to enter Ricco's apartment again, but before she could decide if she should, she heard footsteps down the hall again.

Charlotte looked down the hall and saw Barnaby turn the corner.

"Charlotte! How are you doing? All better from that fall?" Barnaby walked toward her with a ladder under one arm and a light globe clutched in his other hand.

"I'm fine. Thanks Barnaby." Charlotte continued to her apartment.

lly opened the door to the cottage to find her grandmother on the other side.

"Before you start lecturing me, I'm going to stop you right now." Charlotte stepped inside in a bluster of movement and words. "I tried to break into Ricco's apartment, and yes I should have told you. But I couldn't get into his apartment anyway and the key he had outside didn't work. So, there's no use being upset with me. I saw John in the hallway. John always likes to share what he knows, I think it makes him feel important." She crouched down to greet Arnold. The pig licked her hands and grunted as he pranced around her. "Oh yes, I missed you, too, so much." Charlotte kissed the top of his head.

"Mee-Maw!" Ally took a sharp breath. "You told me you were going to rest."

"I said, no lectures." Charlotte looked up at her with a frown. "I couldn't get in anyway, I'm afraid to say."

"We're going to discuss this." Ally met her eyes. "You could have been hurt!"

"Later!" Charlotte explained what John had told her.

"So, according to John, Ricco recently made some

major changes to his will." Ally nodded. "That is a big development."

Peaches jumped down from the couch and wound her way through Charlotte's legs as she purred.

"Hi there, beautiful." Charlotte stroked the cat's fur, then looked up at Ally. "After John left, I thought about trying to get inside the apartment again, but I ran into Barnaby in the hallway. He was headed toward Ricco's apartment with a light globe, so I'm pretty glad I didn't manage to get inside. I might have been caught."

"You should never have even thought about going in there."

"Enough of that."

"What do you think about him changing his will?"

"I'd say Ronaldo had the most motive to commit the crime, knowing what we do now." Charlotte shivered. "To think that Nola would get more than half of Ricco's money, instead of Ronaldo getting all of it. I'm sure if he knew about it, that would have made him furious."

"Absolutely, it would. But could he really do that to his father, knowing how much he loved Nola?"

Ally shook her head as she considered the possibility. "I just don't think so."

"You have to remember, if he is guilty, he's the one who hit Nola over the head with a log hard enough to kill her." Charlotte raised her eyebrows. "That doesn't sound like a person who has a lot of concern for human life, or compassion. Also, keep in mind that if he did attack Nola, there's a good possibility that he had found out about his father changing his will, which might have made him just as angry at Ricco as he was at Nola."

"Mee-Maw, you're right!" Ally gasped as she turned back to face her. "What have we done?"

"What do you mean?" Charlotte frowned as she studied Ally's expression. "Why are you so upset?"

"We let Ricco go home with Ronaldo!" Ally grabbed her purse. "Mee-Maw, we have to go to Ronaldo's house right now!"

"What? Why?" Charlotte followed after her.

"Because if Ricco finds out that it was Ronaldo who killed Nola, then Ronaldo might kill him, too." Ally hurried toward her car. "And even if he doesn't find out, we may have just let Ricco go home with a murderer. A murderer who might have killed his ex-wife in order to secure his inheritance. If he's willing to kill Nola for it, then why wouldn't he follow through and kill his father, too, before he has the chance to find out the truth?"

"Oh Ally!" Charlotte settled in the passenger seat. "I didn't even think of that! If he can murder Nola, you're right, he may just decide he wants to speed up his inheritance and get rid of Ricco, too. But he sounded so protective of his father today."

"He sounded that way, but clearly, he didn't necessarily feel that way. He never visited his father." Ally frowned as she drove down the road. "In my experience a relationship fails for a reason. Maybe things went wrong between Ronaldo and Nola, because Nola figured out that Ronaldo wanted to kill his father to get his inheritance as soon as he could. Maybe that's why she was so concerned about his well-being, and was always coming to visit him."

"You're right." Charlotte nodded as she tapped on her phone. "I'm pulling up Ronaldo's address now. Turn right at the lights, the next one." She looked up as Ally jerked the wheel hard to the right. "Easy Ally, we need to get there in one piece."

"I'm sorry, Mee-Maw, I'm just so worried that we let Ricco go home to be murdered."

"Take a deep breath." Charlotte rubbed her shoulder. "It's not likely that Ronaldo would kill him right away. That would look pretty suspicious, don't you think? He might have lost his temper and killed Nola, and now he has to figure out what his next step will be. If he's the murderer, then he's probably only thinking about staying out of prison right now."

"Let's hope so." Ally followed Charlotte's directions to Ronaldo's home. She noticed that it was quite small, but well-kept. The yard was neat, and the paint looked fresh. It was clear that Ronaldo took some pride in it.

"What's our plan?" Charlotte looked over at Ally as she parked.

"I have no idea, we just need to get in there, and get Ricco back to Freely Lakes, where it's safe." Ally pulled the keys out of the ignition and opened the car door.

The moment Ally stepped out, sharp voices greeted her. She could hear the shouting from the house, even though she was only in the driveway.

CHAPTER 10

"It sounds like we got here just in time!" Charlotte hurried up to the front door. She raised her hand to knock. The door was open slightly but she didn't want to just barge in.

"Wait, Mee-Maw." Ally caught her hand before it could land. "What are they saying? We should listen, just in case Ronaldo says something incriminating."

"Ronaldo, please son, just tell me the truth! Did you hurt Nola? I'm your father, I will find a way to protect you, but you have to tell me the truth!"

"How could you even think that?" Ronaldo shouted back. "What kind of man do you think I am? Before Nola came around, you used to trust me, you used to think I was a good man!"

"Ronaldo, Nola was an angel! She took such good care of me. I know it broke your heart when she left, you just have to tell me the truth."

"I am telling you the truth. She's the one who lied to you. Ever since we got married, she started telling you lies about me. I didn't think it mattered at first, I thought you knew me well enough that you wouldn't believe her. I thought you would see through her lies." Ronaldo shouted. "But you didn't. She turned you against me. You don't even care about your own son anymore."

"I do care about you, Ronaldo. Of course I do." Ricco's voice grew high-pitched as he pleaded. "But how could you say such terrible things about Nola? She was an amazing woman. She was always taking care of me, more than anyone else ever has."

"You don't need taking care of, Dad! She was just babying you. She was just manipulating you to make you trust her more than you trusted me." Ronaldo's voice got even louder.

"That's it!" Ally skipped knocking on the door and threw the door open instead. She stepped inside just as Ronaldo strode toward his father. "Leave him alone, Ronaldo!" She glared at him.

"What are you doing in my house?" Ronaldo

turned toward her, his movements sharp and angry as he approached her.

"Ronaldo, calm down!" Ricco hollered from behind his son. "Your temper is always the problem!"

"Get out of my house!" Ronaldo pointed straight at Ally as he came to a stop a few feet from her. "You have no right to be here!"

"I'm not going anywhere without Ricco!" Ally crossed her arms as she continued to glare at him. She tried to portray a strong attitude but her heart was racing.

"That's right, we think it's better if he comes with us." Charlotte walked over to Ricco and put an arm around his shoulders.

"You're obviously upset with him!" Ally took a step toward him.

"Of course I'm upset with him." Ronaldo laughed, the sound marred by his intense frustration. "If he wants to go, he can of course." He rolled his eyes and threw his hands up in the air. "He doesn't care about me. I've tried long enough to get him to love me." He turned to face Ricco. "I'm not going to be intimidated by a man who thinks I might be a murderer. I had nothing to do with Nola's murder, whether you want to believe me or not. But all that matters to you is that your precious angel is dead. You won't see me shed a single tear over her."

A heavy silence blanketed the room as Ricco and Ronaldo stared at each other.

Ally placed her arm around Ricco's shoulders.

"Let's go. We'll get you back home for the night, alright?"

"Yes." Ricco gazed at his son for a moment longer, then nodded. "Yes, that would be best."

On the drive back to Freely Lakes, Ally glanced over at Ricco in the seat beside her.

"Ricco, are you alright?"

"I will be," Ricco whispered as he stared hard through the windshield.

Charlotte reached up from the back seat to pat his shoulder as she spoke in a gentle tone.

"Everything seems impossible now, but this too shall pass, Ricco."

"I had come to rely on Nola so much. Now, I don't even know if I can trust my son." Ricco shook his head, then closed his eyes. "Never, in all of these years, did it cross my mind that he could do something so terrible. Nothing makes sense right now."

"How did Nola help you?" Charlotte sat back against her seat. "We can make sure that you get the help that you need, even if it's not Nola, you can still get help."

"It wasn't just how she helped me. It was her presence. Her kindness. She cared for me." Ricco squeezed his hands into fists. "Yes, she helped me with all my medicine, and my doctors, but she also danced with me, and played cards with me. She always made sure that I had the food I needed, and everything was clean. She took care of me."

"She sounds like a wonderful person." Ally swallowed hard at the thought of Ricco losing someone so special to him. She wanted to help get justice for an innocent woman that had dedicated her spare time to help someone.

"She was." Ricco lifted one shoulder in a mild shrug. "From what I knew. But she wouldn't ever tell me about herself. Nola and Ronaldo eloped, so no family or friends were invited to the wedding. I'd ask Nola about her family, her past, and she'd dismiss the question, or change the subject. I wish I had insisted. She must have family out there somewhere. There must be other people missing her right now."

"You said she helped you with your medicines and your doctors?" Charlotte scooted forward in her seat again. "That's something I can make sure you get help with. How did Nola help you?"

"My doctors are so frustrated. They can't figure out why I don't get any better, even with all of their treatments. She helped me to make sure I was taking my medicine at the right time and in the right amount. She also gave me supplements and vitamins to help me improve. She cooked for me to be sure that I was eating the right foods to help get control of my blood sugar levels. Sometimes she would come with me to my appointments, which I really appreciated. My doctors talk so fast sometimes, and it's hard for me to keep track of what they're saying. All I know is that every time I go, nothing has improved. I am actually getting worse." Ricco narrowed his eyes. "They act like it's my fault, like I'm doing something wrong. But I am trying. I'm exercising and eating the right things, mostly."

"I'm sorry to hear that. Hopefully, they can help you get better." Charlotte frowned, then met Ally's eyes in the rear view mirror. "We're going to make sure you have what you need. You can always call me if you need anything."

"Thank you." Ricco looked over his shoulder. "I don't know what I'd do without you. I thought I'd always have Ronaldo to rely on. We've always had our issues, but he was still my son. Now—" He turned back to look through the windshield. "Now, I'm not sure that I can call him that."

"He seemed so angry." Ally turned into the parking lot of Freely Lakes. "Is he always like that?"

"He's always had a short temper. I can't blame him. I've always had one, too. But lately it seems to be much worse. The way he behaved tonight was terrible, he was so angry, I've never seen him like that before." Ricco frowned as Ally parked. "If he did hurt Nola, which I don't want to believe, but if he did, I don't think I will ever be able to forgive him. I've loved him since the moment he was born, but that will break my heart. He will no longer be my son in my eyes, he will only be a murderer."

Ally's heart pounded as she helped Ricco out of the car. She wanted to reassure him that his son was innocent. She wanted to give him one good thing to hold onto. But she couldn't. After seeing the way that Ronaldo lost his temper, she believed he was capable of killing Nola, and he had plenty of motive. With Nola out of the picture, Ronaldo probably thought that Ricco would change back the will to leave everything to him. Maybe Ronaldo thought he was still going to inherit the money. Did Ronaldo know about the will being changed?

Ricco settled into an easy chair in his living room.

Charlotte glanced around the room. It was as she remembered it. He kept it very neat, or Nola did. All of his dishes were done, his floors looked freshly vacuumed, and all of the paintings were hung perfectly on the walls. She guessed from the thin layer of dust on some of the shelves, and the scattered framed photographs, that this was one area that he hadn't allowed Nola to straighten up.

Charlotte looked more closely at the photographs. None of them seemed to hold any clues to Ronaldo and Nola's past. But one of them caught her attention and she couldn't help but smile at the sight of Ronaldo, not the blustery, short-tempered giant of a man that she'd seen shortly before, but a toddler in overalls with bright eyes and a cheek to cheek smile.

"Can I get anything for you, Ricco?" Charlotte asked.

"Yes, my medications please. I forgot to take them before I left." Ricco pointed to the bottles on the table. "If you look at the notes on the side you can see that Nola has written out which ones I need to take."

"Sure." Charlotte read through the detailed notes

and got the medication for Ricco. All of the bottles were the same, orange tinted with white labels wrapped around them. But one of the labels didn't have anything printed on it. No doctor's name, no name of the medicine inside, or the dosage that Ricco was supposed to take. "Do you know what this one is for?"

Charlotte showed it to him.

"Oh yes, it's a vitamin." Ricco nodded. "Nola got it specially for me. She said I must have it with the rest of the vitamins."

"Okay." Charlotte opened the bottle. "It's empty."

"Oh, well I don't know where she got it from. When I see the nurse I'll ask her if she knows." Ricco nodded.

"Okay." Charlotte gave him his medication and a glass of water.

After making sure that Ricco wanted her to, Ally checked the refrigerator and freezer, as well as the cabinets, to make sure that he had enough food. When she returned to the living room she sat down across from him.

"Ricco, I know that Ronaldo and Nola fought, but was there any other reason that Ronaldo might have wanted her gone?" Ally looked into his eyes. "Had he found out about anything recently that might have pushed him over the edge?"

"Nothing. I can't think of anything." Ricco shook his head.

Ally frowned. She didn't want to mention that she knew about the will when he was so upset. She also didn't want Ricco to suspect that John had been the one to tell them about it. But she guessed if it was true, that had been the driving force behind Ronaldo's decision to kill his ex-wife.

"There hadn't been any recent changes? Anything that Nola was involved in?" Ally glanced over at her grandmother who carried a cup of tea to Ricco.

"I told you, no." Ricco sighed. "Thank you both for helping me tonight. I'm sorry, I think I just need to be alone to sort through all of this." He sipped his tea, then looked up at Charlotte. "I wish you hadn't been caught up in this, Charlotte."

"I'm sorry you lost someone so special to you." Charlotte hugged him, then nodded to Ally. "Let's let him get some rest." She glanced back at Ricco as she neared the door. "But if you need anything at all, please let me know."

"I will." Ricco sank down farther in the chair. "Thanks again, Charlotte."

Ally stepped out through the door and paused in the hallway as Charlotte closed the door behind her.

"Do you think he's going to be okay?" She frowned as she looked back at the closed door.

"We've done all we can, darling." Charlotte wrapped her arm around Ally's. "I don't think he will be okay again until he knows what happened to Nola. Let's try to focus our energy on trying to help figure it out."

CHAPTER 11

Early the next morning, Charlotte woke up even more determined to find Nola's murderer. She wanted the person caught, so the investigation could be put to rest and justice could be served.

After a quick cup of coffee, Charlotte decided she needed to find out more about Ricco and Nola's relationship. If he and Nola were so close, then he likely held the key to who her murderer was, even if he didn't know it. Ronaldo was an easy choice, but there wasn't enough evidence to prove his involvement, yet. She needed to know more about Nola's life with Ricco, and whether anything stood out about it that might point to the murderer.

Charlotte recalled that Ricco took Cynthia's art

classes. Cynthia was a resident and she ran the class. Maybe Charlotte could see if Cynthia knew anything more about Ricco. Maybe she would know more about his relationship with Nola, if she often saw him.

Charlotte made her way to Cynthia's room. She looked at the decorations around the door and they immediately brought a smile to her lips. There was a Christmas wreath on the door, with a small inflatable Santa on one side of the door and a snowman on the other side. Charlotte knew that Cynthia's grandchildren had given them to her and whenever Charlotte walked past her door they put her in the Christmas spirit. Charlotte knocked on the door. She knew Cynthia would be up despite the early hour.

The door swung open and Cynthia smiled out at her. As Charlotte had predicted she looked like she had been up for hours.

"Charlotte." Her smile widened.

"Cynthia, I'm sorry to bother you so early."

"Oh, it's no trouble. I've been up for a couple of hours already." Cynthia smiled. "Best part of the day. What can I do for you?"

"I wanted to talk to you about Ricco, if you have a few minutes?" Charlotte smiled.

"Sure I do. Such a shame about Nola." Cynthia gestured for her to step inside. "Come inside and I'll make us some coffee."

"Thank you." Charlotte stepped inside and looked around at the paintings on the wall. They were beautiful and all of various landscapes. "You've got some new pieces up?"

"Yes, I've been busy on them." Cynthia called from the kitchen as she made them coffee.

"They are amazing." Charlotte smiled. "You are very talented."

"I try. It is a passion of mine." Cynthia walked in with the coffee, set the cups on the coffee table, then sat in a chair.

Charlotte sat down across from her.

"Ricco must be so heartbroken over Nola's death." Cynthia took a sip of her coffee.

"He is. Did you know Nola well?"

"No, just in passing." Cynthia smiled. "She did come to some of the art classes with Ricco. He often mentioned how Nola helped him. When I checked on him, he said he didn't need anything, Nola took care of everything and he was fine."

"You checked on him?" Charlotte had a sip of coffee.

"I did. He stopped coming to art class. Said he felt

weak, so I checked on him." Cynthia leaned forward. "You see, I'm a doctor. At least, I used to be."

Charlotte's eyes widened. She had no idea that the carefree artist was a doctor.

"I know." Cynthia laughed as she looked at Charlotte's expression. "You wouldn't guess it when you see how I live, now. I used to be much more uptight. I craved a life change, now my main focus is following my passion, relaxing and taking care of myself."

"I had no idea." Charlotte put her coffee cup back down on the table.

"You see, I know Ricco often visited his doctors. As far as I know he has no major illnesses, at least according to him he doesn't. He has a couple of minor ailments and the medicine he is on should be doing its job. But I've watched him getting weaker and weaker. That's why he left art class, he just couldn't do it anymore." Cynthia bit into her bottom lip. "I'm honestly quite worried for him."

"He's weak?" Charlotte took another sip of coffee. "How much strength do you think he has lost?"

"When we used to have coffee at art class he would always pick up the gallon of milk and pour it for me. Then I noticed that all of a sudden he couldn't lift the bottle, so I started buying smaller bottles. He isn't steady on his feet anymore either." Cynthia shook her head. "I went to see him to try and convince him to visit a different doctor. But he insisted he had seen a couple that Nola had organized for him and they were doing what they could."

"But you thought something was wrong?" Charlotte asked.

"I did. I was worried about him." Cynthia frowned as she took her last sip of coffee.

"I'm not surprised. Maybe you can convince him to see a different doctor, now that Nola isn't around."

"I'm going to try." Cynthia looked toward her phone as it buzzed with an alarm. She reached over and turned it off. "Sorry, about that. That's to remind me to start my morning walk."

"No problem. I should be on my way. Enjoy your walk." Charlotte stood up and walked toward the door. Before she reached it, she stopped and turned back. "Sorry, one more question. Did you ever talk to Nola about how she was taking care of Ricco?"

"I praised her for it. One time, I asked her about the vitamins and supplements she was giving Ricco. I was interested in what she had him on, as nothing seemed to be helping him. He was getting worse. She told me all about them. Some of it was pointless, but none of it would do any harm. She told me she just wanted to keep Ricco around as long as she could. She did seem to care about him." Cynthia's lips pursed as she glanced away from her, then shook her head. "I still can't believe that someone killed her."

"It's hard to fathom." Charlotte waited until Cynthia looked back at her. "Did you ever notice any tension between Nola and Ricco, or maybe with his son, Ronaldo?"

"Not at all." Cynthia frowned. "Nola was always fawning over him, and he seemed happy to receive the attention."

"Thanks for the coffee, Cynthia." Charlotte smiled at her. "Hopefully, we can get together again soon."

"That sounds lovely." Cynthia smiled. "Take care of yourself, Charlotte."

With Cynthia's words still echoing through her mind, Charlotte headed down the hall, back toward her apartment. She focused on what Cynthia had to say about Ricco's health. If he really was as weak as she claimed, there was no way that he could have picked up a log and used it to kill Nola. That didn't rule him out completely from working with

Ronaldo, but with no motive to kill Nola, and his rocky relationship with his son, she couldn't think of a reason why the pair would team up to kill Nola.

❧

*A*lly opened the side door to the kitchen in the chocolate shop and smiled as her grandmother stepped through it.

"Morning, Mee-Maw, thanks for coming in."

"Absolutely. I know what the Christmas season is like. How are you doing on the mail orders? They have to be out by tomorrow." Charlotte brushed past her and headed straight for the boxes of candy stacked on the shelves.

"I received a few last minute orders first thing this morning, so I'm finishing those up." Ally walked over to the long, stainless steel table and began taking candies off of several trays to fill a box.

"It sounds like you're on top of it, I'm impressed." Charlotte pulled on an apron and stepped up beside her. "How can I help?"

"I need a full box of cherry cordials." Ally added a few nut clusters to the box, then moved onto the next one.

Charlotte put on gloves and began filling up the

box of cherry cordials as she described her conversation with Cynthia.

"From her description of Ricco's health, I think we can rule him out as a suspect."

"It's good to eliminate Ricco as a suspect." Ally released a heavy sigh. "I was hoping he wasn't the one who did this to Nola, after all she did to help him. Plus, it wouldn't make sense for him to kill her since apparently he changed his will to leave more than half his fortune to her, he obviously cared for her."

"That part surprises me a little." Charlotte shook her head. "I know that Ricco said he was close with Nola and that she made him feel as if he had a family again, but he still had Ronaldo. Why wouldn't he give more to Ronaldo, or at least split it evenly between them? Ronaldo is his son, after all. Don't you think it's a little odd that he wanted to leave her more than him?"

"Maybe." Ally finished stacking the packages of candy. "But maybe he felt so resentful of Ronaldo, he just didn't want to leave him as much as Nola. It's certainly possible. Either way, we know that Ricco couldn't have killed Nola at this point. The question is, who does that leave us as suspects?"

"Ronaldo, of course." Charlotte wiped down the

counter as she looked toward the front door. "The ladies are here already."

"Of course, they are." Ally grinned as she walked toward the door. "It doesn't matter what time we actually open, they will always be first in line." She unlocked the door and waved the three women inside. "Good morning, Mrs. Cale, Mrs. White, and Mrs. Bing."

"Ally, are we early?" Mrs. White eyed the front door. "I didn't expect it to still be locked."

"We're a bit swamped this morning." Ally shrugged as she decided not to mention that they were a few minutes early. "So, we hadn't gotten around to unlocking the door just yet. How are you?"

"Terrible, just terrible." Mrs. Bing walked right up to the front counter and plucked a candy from the sample tray. She dropped it into her mouth, closed her eyes, and sighed. "That's better."

"Me next." Mrs. Cale stepped up behind her.

"What's wrong?" Charlotte looked at Mrs. White. "Did something happen?"

"Oh, we're just trying to sort through all of this darkness, right before Christmas." Mrs. White clucked her tongue. "All anyone wants to talk about is the murder. All of the festivities we have planned have a dark cloud over them now. People are canceling left and right because they are afraid to attend. Rumor is that the murderer is on the hunt for another victim."

"What?" Ally's eyes widened. "Where is that rumor coming from? Luke thinks the killer likely had a personal motive to kill Nola. It wasn't random. Which means that most likely no one else is in danger."

"So you say, but everyone else is claiming it's a Christmas serial killer and we all need to lock ourselves away before we're next." Mrs. Cale shuddered. "I almost didn't come here today. But you know I can't miss my morning chocolate and coffee."

"Here it is." Charlotte placed a mug down in front of her. "I'm so sorry you three are frightened by all of this. But you really shouldn't listen to those rumors."

"Frightened?" Mrs. White picked up her coffee. "I wouldn't say that. Enraged, is more accurate for me. I am just so angry that whoever the killer is, did this at the most joyful time of the year. How inconsiderate."

"I am frightened." Mrs. Cale sipped her coffee, then shivered. "I was there you know, likely right when the murder took place. I can't shake the idea that it could have easily been me instead of Nola."

"You were there?" Ally's eyes widened. "I didn't know that. Were you visiting a friend?"

"The hairstylist actually. Her name is Janene. She's fantastic. I have a standing appointment with her once a month in her salon in the center of Freely. But she had to cancel on me at the last minute the day before, so she offered to see me at Freely Lakes instead. She's there for a few hours a week. I didn't mind because I could see my friend Rhonda afterward." Mrs. Cale shook her head. "Now, I don't even want to think about going back to see Rhonda, at least not until this murderer is caught."

"It's always good to be cautious." Ally met her grandmother's eyes, then set a tray of candies down in front of the three women. "But we can't let fear rule our lives either. How was your appointment with Janene?"

"Not great." Mrs. Cale sighed. "She seemed distracted, even after arriving late. The appointment was supposed to be at eleven and she didn't get there until ten after."

"Oh?" Ally's heart skipped a beat as she knew that the time of death was estimated to be around eleven, and her grandmother had found Nola's body at eleven fifteen. "Did she seem scared?"

"Scared?" Mrs. Cale shook her head. "No. She apologized. She said she had to grab a coffee in the lobby. She woke up late and hadn't had time to make one at home that morning. So, that was her first coffee for the day." She scrunched up her nose. "People today don't take punctuality very seriously." She raised her eyebrows as she looked at Ally.

Ally's cheeks burned. Mrs. Cale obviously counted her among those people, since the door to the shop hadn't been unlocked when she arrived.

"Did she leave the salon at all after she arrived?" Charlotte set out cream and sugar for their coffee.

"No, she stayed until my hair was done. By then all of the commotion had started." Mrs. Cale fluffed the sharp edge of her bob. "I think she did a pretty good job this time. She can be a bit heavy handed with the scissors on occasion."

"It looks very nice." Mrs. Bing smiled as she patted her own hair. "I might have to make an appointment myself." She took a sharp breath. "In town of course. I won't go to Freely Lakes again, not until after the murderer is caught, of course." She popped a candy from the sample tray in her mouth.

"Although, it might be worth going there to find out more information."

"It might be." Mrs. Cale frowned. "The faster that horrible person is behind bars the better." She locked her eyes to Ally's. "When is Luke going to make that happen?"

"Remember, he is only assisting in Freely, but I'm sure that they will have it solved soon enough." Ally pulled out her phone and sent a quick text to Luke about Janene. As she tucked it back into her pocket she met Mrs. White's eyes. "They're all working hard to find the truth."

"Even if they do, it may be too late to save Christmas." Mrs. White picked up a candy. "No one wants to celebrate when something like murder occurs."

"On the contrary, I think it makes us all hold onto our loved ones a little tighter." Charlotte placed her hand over Mrs. White's. "And value the time we have to spend with them. I do hope you still plan to join us for dinner."

"I wouldn't miss it." Mrs. White smiled. "Especially, if you'll have one of your delicious chocolate Yule logs there."

"Absolutely." Charlotte grinned. "Plenty for everyone."

"Break time." Ally sank down into a chair in the kitchen.

"Now, that we're caught up on the orders, where are we with the investigation?"

"We have spoken to the person she was closest to at Freely Lakes, Ricco, and that didn't tell us much." Ally crossed her legs as she sat back in her chair. "But we haven't really combed through her activities that day. Maybe something that happened to her that morning, or the day before, led to her death. There could be a clue there."

"Funny you should say that. I heard through the grapevine that someone saw Nola speak with Barnaby and the manager Albert, the afternoon before her death. She also visited a few of Ricco's neighbors that afternoon and evening." Charlotte smiled. "Apparently, she was questioning the neighbors about things that had been stolen from their apartments."

"Interesting. She was conducting an investigation of her own?" Ally nodded. "That makes sense, actually. She was very protective of Ricco."

"She probably wanted to figure out who the thief was, so that Ricco would be safer." Charlotte narrowed her eyes.

"Which means there's a chance Nola did find out who the thief was, and then confronted that person." Ally's eyes widened. "If she got the information she needed from one of the people she spoke to, then there is a chance we could get that same information from talking to them. Maybe they will feel more comfortable speaking to us, or maybe something else will have surfaced in their memories."

"Retracing her steps, that's a great idea." Charlotte stood up. "I'll start on the people she apparently spoke to, right away."

"Mee-Maw, you're not doing this alone. The shop is closing in a few minutes anyway. I can take a couple of hours off." Ally walked toward the door.

"During the Christmas rush? Ally, I'm not sure

that's a good idea." Charlotte frowned. "Don't you have lots of orders to fill?"

"I'm actually keeping up pretty well. All of the mail orders are ready to go, and the shelves are stocked with back-up boxes. We're going to be fine. You have been a huge help. I can come in later and make up time." Ally turned the lock on the front door and flipped the sign to closed. "I'm not letting you do this alone, so you might as well not argue with me."

"Oh, I know that stubborn streak when I hear it." Charlotte rolled her eyes. "Alright, let's start with some of the neighbors."

Ally walked toward the back door. "Let me check on Peaches and Arnold, first." She stepped out through the back door.

"I'd love to see those rascals." Charlotte headed through the door right behind her.

Arnold bolted straight to her, snorting and tail wagging happily.

"Hi baby." Charlotte nuzzled his cheek and hugged him. "You are so sweet. I miss you, too." She laughed as Arnold licked her cheek.

Peaches jumped down from the wall that was there more to keep Arnold in, than the cat. Peaches was becoming quite the escape artist and often managed to escape and roam the neighborhood, getting treats from every friendly neighbor.

"Look at you!" Ally stroked the cat's fur. "What have you been getting into?" She laughed as she pulled a few leaves off of the tip of her tail.

"Trouble, I'm sure." Charlotte eyed her with a smile. "She's always up to something."

~

When Charlotte and Ally arrived at Freely Lakes, Charlotte noticed a few police cars in the parking lot. It was an unusual sight, as things were generally calm.

"I wonder what they are doing here? Maybe there's been a break in the case?"

"Luke said the manager requested a few police officers stay close, until more is known about the killer. I guess he wants to be sure that the residents feel safe." Ally stepped out of the car.

"Smart move." Charlotte led the way to the apartment of one of the people she had heard Nola spoke to. "Rhonda is a bit of a stickler when it comes to rules, but generally she is easy to get along with." She knocked sharply on the door.

The door swung open swiftly, a short woman

with bright red curls that matched her lipstick poked her head out into the hall.

"Charlotte, it's so nice to see you." Rhonda eyed Charlotte's hands. "Oh, I had hoped you might have some chocolate with you."

"Here you go." Ally smiled as she pulled a small box of candy from her purse. "Just for you."

"Thank you, that's so sweet of you." Rhonda grinned. "You're Ally, right? Your grandmother never stops talking about you!"

"Is that so?" Ally laughed, then glanced at her grandmother.

"Just about the wedding, and how great you are doing with the shop." Charlotte waved her hand. "Rhonda, can we come in for a moment?"

"Of course." Rhonda gestured for them to step inside. "You two are always welcome. I have to be more cautious now, with a killer on the loose."

"That's what we'd like to talk to you about." Charlotte followed her into a small living room with two pristine couches. "When was the last time you saw Nola?"

"Oh, the night before she was killed." Rhonda settled on one of the couches and frowned. "I didn't expect to see her, but I did."

"So, she came looking for you?" Charlotte

watched as the woman glanced up at her, then looked away quickly.

"Yes, she did." Rhonda cleared her throat.

"Rhonda, we're just trying to help figure out what she might have been up to that day." Ally offered her a reassuring smile. "That's all."

"I understand." Rhonda took a shaky breath. "But I just can't help feeling responsible."

"Responsible?" Charlotte narrowed her eyes. "For what?"

"For Nola's death." Rhonda's voice broke as tears welled up in her eyes. "I just feel so terrible. I wish I had never opened my door that night."

"Slow down, Rhonda." Charlotte stood up and walked over to her. She picked up a box of tissues and offered them to her, as Rhonda began to sob. "What do you mean? Why would it have mattered if you didn't open the door?"

"I wasn't going to." Rhonda snatched a few tissues from the box and pressed them against one eye, then the other. "It was getting late and I didn't know who it was. But I opened it, and there she was. I knew who she was, because Ricco and I would play cards together, and sometimes Nola would join us. She said she knew that some things had gone missing from my apartment and she just wanted to ask me a few questions about it." She took a deep breath. "She said she just wanted to help."

Ally glanced at her grandmother, then looked back at Rhonda. "How did she want to help?"

"She told me that she suspected who might be stealing from the residents. But she needed a little more information before she could confront him." Rhonda looked down at her hands, then took a sharp breath. "I never should have said a word! If I hadn't, she might still be alive!"

"Oh Rhonda." Charlotte rubbed her shoulder as she sat down beside her on the couch. "Sweetheart, this wasn't your fault."

"Wasn't it?" Rhonda shook her head. "If I hadn't told her what I did, she might not have confronted the thief, and he might not have killed her."

"You know who the thief is?" Ally's voice sharpened.

"I told her who I suspected. Who I saw in the hallway near where one of the thefts occurred." Rhonda shook her head. "I hadn't told anybody. I didn't want any trouble. But she was so determined that she could help, and I wanted the thief caught."

"Who was it?" Charlotte took her hand and gave it a gentle squeeze. "You can tell us. No one will ever find out who told us."

"Charlotte, I didn't tell the police who it was. What happens if I get into trouble?" Rhonda squeezed her eyes shut tight. "I don't want to get into trouble because I was keeping information from the police."

"It's okay. You can tell us. You won't get into trouble." Ally looked into her eyes. "The most important thing is that you tell the truth now."

Rhonda took a sharp breath.

"It was Barnaby. It was late at night, I couldn't sleep. I decided to just go outside and get a breath of fresh air. But when I stepped out into the hall, I saw Barnaby leaving Adeline's apartment. He didn't see me, but I saw him. I thought it was very strange for him to be there so late at night. The next day she said that she hadn't been home, and some of her jewelry had been stolen." Rhonda stared down at Charlotte's hand wrapped around hers. "I didn't want to believe it. I guess that's why I never told anyone. But Nola got the truth out of me. I can only think she confronted Barnaby, and he killed her." She looked up at Charlotte, her eyes glistening with tears. "So, how is it not my fault?"

"It's not your fault." Charlotte stared straight into her eyes. "It's going to be okay."

Ally already had her phone out as she stepped out

of the apartment. As she waited for Luke to answer, Charlotte frowned.

"Barnaby. It makes sense that it would be him. If he is the thief, then there is a good chance he is also the murderer."

Ally nodded, then began to speak into the phone. After she explained what they found out, she requested that one of the officers keep an eye on Rhonda's room.

"He's going to make sure that someone is close to this apartment all night." She tucked the phone back into her pocket.

"Do you think she's in real danger?" Charlotte looked back at the closed door.

"I doubt it. I can understand her concern, though. At this point, we don't know for sure that the thief is also the murderer, but we certainly can't rule it out." Ally raised an eyebrow.

"From what I heard, Rhonda was not the last person that Nola spoke to that night. If she suspected Barnaby, then why did she go speak to someone else before confronting him?"

"That's a good point." Ally nodded. "Maybe she wanted more proof it was him."

"From what I heard, Daniel was the last person

she spoke to that night?" Charlotte started down the hall.

"It's possible she spoke to someone else after him, isn't it?"

"It is, but I haven't heard about it." Charlotte shook her head. "Barnaby does seem like the perfect suspect in the thefts. There haven't been any signs of forced entry." She continued down the hallway, each step delivered with determination. "He'd have keys and access to all of the apartments."

"But wouldn't he know that would make him the main suspect?" Ally quickened her pace to keep up with her. "Wouldn't he realize the risk he was taking?"

"Maybe he hoped that no one would notice. He'd just take a few things, maybe he thought the residents wouldn't miss them. Maybe he thought it would just be presumed that they had made a mistake and they were being forgetful." Charlotte shrugged as she stopped in front of an apartment door. "We might be able to find out more from Daniel. I've seen him and Barnaby spending time together more than once. It seems to me they might be friends." She knocked on the door.

CHAPTER 13

The man who opened the door took a slight step back at the sight of them. "Charlotte, of all the people I expected to be on the other side of my door, you're not one of them."

"Sorry to disturb you, Daniel, do you mind if we come in for a few minutes?" Charlotte studied his shocked expression. "Are you busy?"

"No, not busy." Daniel took a breath, then shook his head. "I'm sorry, I just don't know what to say to you, Charlotte, after what you went through."

"Never mind that. I'm fine. There are more important things to discuss." Charlotte brushed past him into his apartment.

Ally followed a few steps behind her.

"What things?" Daniel closed the door behind

them, then turned to face them. "Are you talking about Nola?"

"She came to see you the night before she was killed." Charlotte watched his expression shift from shock to worry.

"I spoke to the police about that already." Daniel walked farther into the apartment and sighed. "I don't think I want to go over it all again."

"We'd just like to know what she came to talk to you about." Charlotte paused a few steps behind him. "Can you tell us that?"

"She came to talk to me about a terrible crime." Daniel turned to face them, the muscles in his face taut. "It's exactly what I don't want to discuss."

"You had something stolen from your apartment?" Ally eased a little closer to him. "I'm sure that was very upsetting."

"Is very upsetting." Daniel frowned. "It still is. Losing my cat, was the worst thing that ever happened to me."

"Someone stole your cat?" Ally gasped. "I can't imagine how I would feel if someone stole my cat!"

"It wasn't a real cat." Daniel frowned. "But I loved it just as much. It was my most prized possession." He sighed as he looked over at an empty spot in the center of a lighted shelf. "I never thought it would be at risk in my own home. Although, it's very valuable, it means even more to me than just that. My father and I would hunt antiques together. This was the last item we found together, in the back of a thrift shop. No one there knew what it was worth, but we did. It was like finding lost treasure. Ever since I lost him, seeing that cat reminds me of that moment we shared, and it's like he's right here with me again. At least it was." He took a shaky breath. "Not anymore."

"Did you ever talk to Barnaby about how much it was worth?" Charlotte glanced over the other items on the shelf, an assortment of statues and a few wooden boxes.

"Barnaby?" Daniel shook his head. "No, not that I can recall. He's fond of that." He pointed to a copper ship perched high on a bookshelf. "It's not really worth anything, but he liked the way it caught the sunlight. He's commented on it a few times." He shrugged. "But if you're thinking that Barnaby had anything to do with this, not a chance. He's like family around here. He would never steal from any of us."

"But he did have access." Charlotte raised an eyebrow as she looked back at him. "He has keys to all of the apartments."

"Maybe, but that was only so that he could help

us out if we needed something. I think a few other staff members have keys to the apartments, too. It would look pretty obvious if one of them broke in." Daniel crossed his arms as he stared at Charlotte. "Don't drag him into this. He's an innocent man. He wouldn't cause any harm to anyone."

"How can you be so certain of that?" Ally narrowed her eyes. "Because he was friendly to you?"

"Because he told me how much he loved his family." Daniel lowered his eyes. "We swapped stories, me about losing my father, and him about losing his mother. He was heartbroken and just a little lonely." He waved his hand as he stepped back. "I really don't have anything more to say about any of this."

Ally exchanged a look with her grandmother before she nodded.

"Thanks for your time, Daniel."

~

"Something felt strange about that conversation." Charlotte rubbed a hand along her forearm as she walked along the hallway in the direction of the manager's office. "Don't you think?"

"It seemed to me that Daniel was more interested in protecting Barnaby than finding out who the thief is, or the killer." Ally shook her head. "Maybe they are such good friends he didn't want to cast any suspicion on him."

"Maybe." Charlotte pursed her lips. "But I would think he would want the murderer and thief caught so that Freely Lakes can be crime free. Why would he want to prevent that from happening?"

"Maybe he really believes that Barnaby is innocent. I'm guessing that Nola suspected him and tried to get Daniel to confirm her suspicions. I'd bet that didn't go well." Ally met her grandmother's eyes. "Maybe Daniel is the one that tipped Barnaby off about Nola's suspicions. If he told Barnaby that Nola was close to having him arrested, maybe it wasn't Nola that confronted Barnaby at all, maybe Barnaby confronted her."

Charlotte's eyes widened. "Oh Ally, I hadn't considered that. You might be right. He might have heard Nola and Ricco arguing in the common room. Once he knew where she was all he had to do was wait until no one else was in the common room."

"Do you think he planned to kill her?" Ally frowned. "Or maybe just scare her?"

"I'm not sure. But whatever happened between the two of them in that room led to Nola's death. Hopefully, Albert can give us some actual proof that Barnaby was involved." Charlotte pushed the door open to the office.

Albert hung up the phone as the two stepped inside.

"Whatever it is, it's going to have to wait until later I'm afraid."

"We just have a few questions for you, Albert." Charlotte squared her shoulders as she met his eyes. "They can't wait."

"I'm a little busy putting out fires at the moment." Albert frowned as the phone on his desk began to ring again. "Everyone is demanding that I find out what happened to Nola, as if I have a badge. I certainly don't. I'm just a manager."

"Of course, but I'm sure you can understand why everyone wants the killer caught." Ally sat down in the chair across from his desk. She leaned against the back of it, as she met Albert's eyes. "And it is your responsibility to make sure this complex is as secure as possible."

"I know that, and I take that responsibility very

seriously." Albert shook his head as he pressed a button on the phone to silence the ring. "But nothing is going to change the fact that I don't have any answers about what happened to Nola. So, if that is what you are here for, you are wasting your time."

"Actually, we're here to talk about Barnaby." Charlotte stepped closer to his desk. "It won't take much time for you to answer a few of our questions. I'm sure that you want to be as supportive as you can be to the community here."

"Alright, fine." Albert rolled his eyes. "What do you want to know about Barnaby?"

"Do you trust him?" Charlotte locked eyes with him.

"Trust him?" Albert gave a short laugh. "Of course not. He is a liar."

"What makes you say that?" Ally took a sharp breath.

"Not long after I took over as manager here, I caught him covering up for people with cats. We have a strict no pet policy." Albert frowned.

"I'm aware." Charlotte shook her head. "It's extreme if you ask me." She knew what it was like not to have your pet by your side every day even though she only had to leave Arnold with Ally and could visit whenever she wanted.

"It's the rule here. No pets. It's always been the rule. Cats are the worst. They destroy things, pee everywhere, I can't stand them." Albert shuddered. "So, when I found out that he was helping a few residents hide their cats from me, I was livid. I would have fired him, but he is so well-liked around here that I knew I would face a revolt." He sighed. "I did warn him that he had to watch himself, that I wouldn't tolerate another problem with him."

"Is it really so terrible for someone to have a pet?" Charlotte shook her head. "People enjoy having a companion."

"Whether or not it is terrible is not the point." Albert frowned. "It's against the rules, and he knew that. If people around here didn't like him so much, I would have let him go already."

"Is that what you two were arguing about yesterday?" Ally crossed her arms as she settled her gaze on him. "Did you want to fire him?"

"I don't know what you're talking about." Albert's face paled.

"No?" Charlotte tapped her fingertips on his desk. "It was a pretty loud argument. I couldn't quite make out what was said, though. Could you, Ally?"

"Just bits and pieces." Ally shrugged as she narrowed her eyes. "But it certainly was loud."

"As I said, everyone is tense right now." Albert gestured to the door. "I have a lot of work to do."

"Just one more question." Ally peered at the papers scattered across his desk. "Where is Barnaby now?"

"I have no idea. If you come across him, please let him know that I'm looking for him." Albert gestured to the door again.

Ally met Charlotte's eyes, then walked toward the door.

The moment they were out in the hall, she turned to her grandmother.

"We need to find Barnaby. We know that Nola was angry with him over him not changing a light bulb in Ricco's room. Maybe he thought that was the last straw that would get him fired."

"Or her finding out about him stealing from the residents." Charlotte shook her head. "Just because he was well-liked, doesn't mean he wasn't stealing. Either possibility could be a motive. But until we find Barnaby and talk to him about it, I don't think we're going to get much further."

"I'll check in with Luke. Let's see if he has spoken to Barnaby recently. Let's go to your apartment, though, I don't want anyone listening in to what we know so far." Ally led the way toward her grandmother's apartment. Once there she pulled out her phone and noticed several messages with new orders for the shop and a few from friends about Holiday plans. "Mee-Maw, maybe we should think about canceling our Christmas dinner plans." She frowned as she settled on the couch. "We might not have time to prepare for a big meal with all of this going on."

"Don't you worry about that. Christmas always has a way of working itself out, no matter what kind of chaos is happening around it." Charlotte tipped her head toward her phone. "Just give Luke a call, the sooner we get this settled, the better."

Ally dialed Luke's number and felt some relief as he answered right away.

"I'm a little busy right now, Ally, is everything okay?"

She quickly filled him in on the information they'd discovered.

"If he is the thief, he may also be the murderer. Have you spoken to Barnaby recently. We haven't been able to find him. And from what we can tell, no one seems to have seen him recently." Ally frowned as she listened to the noise in the background. "It sounds a little crazy over there."

"It's busy." Luke sighed, then cleared his throat.

"Okay, I wanted to speak to him again but I haven't managed to find him. I'll see what I can do about tracking him down. I have his home address, so if I can't find him, maybe I'll swing by there to check on things."

"Thanks Luke."

"I want to make sure that this murder is solved, so Charlotte and everyone at Freely Lakes can feel safe again. Just be careful, anyone could be the murderer."

Ally smiled at the determination in his voice. She had no doubt that he would follow through on exactly what he said. Luke had such a protective nature.

Ally ended the call and felt a flutter in her heart. Soon he would be her husband. They would get to spend the rest of their lives together. Something that at one time she thought would never happen. She had been married and divorced and never thought she wanted to get married again. Now, she couldn't wait for it to happen. She pushed away thoughts of the wedding, and what their lives would be like after it, and tried to focus instead on the investigation.

"Luke is going to go by Barnaby's place in the morning to check on him." Ally glanced at her watch. "I think I'm going to go home and get an early start in the morning. Hopefully, Luke finds Barnaby and can speak to him."

"I'll come help you in the morning." Charlotte stood up and walked toward the door.

"I want you to take a break. Take the day off." Ally hugged her grandmother. "I'll be fine with the orders, I promise. If I get too backed up, I'll let you know."

"Maybe I will have a bit of a break and have the day off." Charlotte hugged her back. "Please let me know if you hear anything new from Luke."

"I will."

The following morning, Ally woke up to something pressing down on her arm. She turned to see Arnold's snout resting on her arm. His large round eyes staring at her.

"Morning!" Ally laughed. He snorted. She felt Peaches nestled against her back. "I have to start early today. Thanks for waking me up."

Ally spent a few minutes enjoying their company, then she got ready and headed for the shop.

She spent the morning playing catch up with the new orders between serving customers, but her thoughts lingered on Barnaby. Luke had called her to say hello and let her know that he still hadn't been able to contact him. Why was Barnaby suddenly so difficult to find? Had he taken off to evade being caught? She recalled the man's presence not long after the murder. Would he really come back to the scene of the crime after murdering someone?

A knock on the window that faced the street interrupted her thoughts. Ally wiped her hands on her apron then headed for the front of the shop. She smiled as she saw the three ladies waving to her through the glass.

Mrs. Bing, Mrs. Cale, and Mrs. White pointed to the front door of the shop, then walked away from the window.

She stepped behind the counter in the same moment that the three women stepped in through the front door.

"Oh, it's getting so chilly out there!" Mrs. Bing rubbed her hands together and shivered. "I know we all dream of a white Christmas, but I for one wouldn't mind a tropical one instead."

"Not me." Mrs. White unwrapped her scarf from around her neck. "I love the cold."

"I'm not sure if I love the cold, or the feeling of walking into a nice warm place." Mrs. Cale shrugged off her coat. "It's only during the winter that we get to feel that, isn't it? It's like getting a big, warm hug."

"I've never thought of it that way, Mrs. Cale." Ally

smiled as she walked around the counter to give them each a hug. "But you're absolutely right."

"I cannot wait for a coffee." Mrs. Bing shook her head.

"You didn't come in this morning?" Ally put three coffees on the counter.

"We were helping decorate the hospital. We tried to get here first but there just wasn't enough time." Mrs. Bing pouted. "We haven't had any coffee yet today. You know we need at least two cups of coffee a day during the winter."

"Yes, it's the coffee that we need." Mrs. White laughed as she selected a piece of candy from the sample tray.

"You don't have any white chocolate coconut truffles." Mrs. Cale scanned the tray.

"I'm sorry about that. I didn't make enough, but I will make more so you can have some tomorrow." Ally shook her head. "Between the Christmas orders and trying to figure out what happened to Nola, I've been a little scattered."

"Any news on that?" Mrs. White sat down on one of the stools and watched Ally prepare a pot of coffee.

"Unfortunately, nothing solid. Do any of you

know Barnaby, the maintenance man at Freely Lakes?" Ally turned back to face them.

"I've seen him around when I visited friends." Mrs. Bing made sure her elaborate hat was at the correct angle. "But I've never really spoken to him."

"Can't say that I've ever met him." Mrs. White shrugged, as she grabbed a chocolate from the tray.

"Is it him?" Mrs. Cale's eyes widened. "Is he the murderer?"

"Of course not." Mrs. White huffed. "Everyone knows it was Ronaldo. His own father doesn't even trust him. I wouldn't put it past him to make it look like it was someone else, though." She smiled as she accepted a mug of coffee from Ally.

"Everyone knows that?" Ally raised an eyebrow. "Have any of these people come up with any evidence to prove that?"

"Oh, now you sound like Luke." Mrs. White laughed. "Anytime I call in a tip to him, he is always asking me what proof I have. Really, it's quite exhausting."

"It's important to have proof, though, if you're going to accuse someone of murder." Ally narrowed her eyes. "What are your instincts telling you?"

"My instincts are telling me that marriage doesn't always end on a good note, and that Ronaldo had a lot to lose thanks to his ex-wife cuddling up to his father." Mrs. White sipped her coffee. "Case closed, in my opinion." She popped a candy into her mouth.

~

Ally's thoughts shifted to Ronaldo as she finished up the last of the Christmas orders. She'd just turned the lock on the front door when she heard a knock at the back door. Startled, she hesitated for just a moment. Why would anyone be knocking at the back door instead of the front?

Ally made her way to the door and peered outside. The sight of her grandmother made her sigh with relief. As she unlocked the door she smiled.

"Mee-Maw, what are you doing here? You're supposed to be taking a break."

"I'm done taking a break." Charlotte shook her head. "I think we need to take a fresh look at things. We've become so stuck on the idea that Barnaby did this, but we do have other suspects."

"Like Ronaldo?" Ally grinned. "Mrs. White got to me, too."

"I just finished talking to her on the phone." Charlotte shook her head. "She's pretty convinced."

"I think it's worth looking into. As far as I know,

Luke hasn't been able to locate Barnaby, so for the moment Ronaldo is our best lead. We could head over to his place and try to talk to him again now that he's had some time to calm down." Ally pulled off her apron and hung it up.

"I think that's a great idea." Charlotte nodded. "I've already been by to check on Peaches and Arnold and make sure they had plenty to eat. All that talk about not having pets made me miss their sweet faces."

"Thanks Mee-Maw, I bet they were so happy to see you." Ally locked the door behind her. "Hopefully, Ronaldo will be home."

"And calmer." Charlotte winced as she walked up to Ally's car. "I'll drive, I'm sure you could use a break."

"Thanks Mee-Maw." Ally gave her the keys, then settled in the passenger seat and closed her eyes for the length of time it took to get to Ronaldo's house. When the car pulled to a stop, she jolted awake.

"Ally, are you okay?" Charlotte pushed a few strands of hair away from her granddaughter's cheek.

"I'm okay now, Mee-Maw. I just needed a little rest." Ally stepped out of the car and frowned as she looked at the driveway. "His car isn't here."

"It might still be worth a look around." Charlotte started up the driveway. "Maybe we can spot something incriminating through the windows."

"No, Mee-Maw, we shouldn't." Ally caught her arm and tipped her head toward the neighboring yard. "We're being watched."

"Can I help you two?" A man who appeared to be in his sixties tossed a shovel from hand to hand, his eyes settled on them.

"We were just looking for Ronaldo. Have you seen him?" Ally smiled as she walked toward him.

"I haven't, no." He eyed them both, then leaned heavily on his shovel. "My guess is that he is probably at his favorite bar, Tara's Tavern."

"Oh, thanks." Ally glanced at her grandmother. "I guess we could check there."

"I wouldn't recommend it." He straightened up and looked between the two of them. "It's not a place for nice ladies like you."

"No?" Charlotte raised an eyebrow. "Kind of shady is it?"

"Extremely. Perfect for a guy like Ronaldo, but not for the two of you." He tipped his head to the side. "Why are you looking for him anyway? Trying to put him on the straight and narrow?"

"Not exactly." Charlotte laughed. "We're just

trying to learn a little bit more about him, and his ex-wife, Nola."

"Oh, Nola." His shoulders slumped as he glanced away from them. "Yes, I heard about that. Heartbreaking isn't it? She was so young."

"Did you know her well?" Ally moved a little closer to him as he leaned the shovel against the side of the house.

"No, not well. They weren't married long. But I knew the moment she moved in. The place started getting cleaned up real fast. Ronaldo didn't do much to take care of the house, but once Nola moved in, she had him out mowing and trimming all of the time. They even painted the place." He shrugged. "I thought it was a real good thing for him to have someone that pushed him to do better. Everything seemed to be going well, until they weren't."

"What do you mean by that?" Charlotte crossed her arms. "Did they start arguing?"

"Screaming is more like it." He rolled his eyes. "This is a quiet neighborhood. Most people are respectful to each other. We don't mow the lawn before nine, and we don't blast loud music at parties. So, when those two started fighting, I think everyone in the neighborhood could hear it. I said to him once, can't you keep your business a little more private, and of course that made me a bad guy." He rolled his eyes. "But what can you do? You can't choose your neighbors."

"Do you remember what they were fighting about?" Ally pulled out her phone, prepared to document what he had to say.

"Not really." He rubbed a hand along his chin. "I'd like to say it was all Ronaldo's fault, I'm not a big fan of the guy. But honestly, I think it was Nola that changed. When she first moved in, I only ever saw her being sweet to Ronaldo. But toward the end she was always giving him a hard time. Almost like she wanted to fight. Maybe she just got tired of putting up with him, I don't know. Some of the fights were so bad I thought about calling the police."

"Did you ever see Ronaldo hurt her? Or threaten her?" Ally's fingers flew across the keyboard on her phone, but she glanced up at him to be sure she didn't miss a single word.

"Ronaldo?" He snorted. "No, I didn't see him lift a hand to her. But Nola? She was a spirited one. She'd grab anything nearby and fling it at him. I once saw her toss a flower pot at his head!"

"Wow, did it hit him?" Ally frowned as she tried to picture the scene.

"No, he dodged it." He shook his head. "But I'll

tell you, that's not what love is supposed to look like, not in my opinion. I was relieved to find out they broke up." His grip tightened on his shovel. "I have to get back to work."

"Thanks for the information." Charlotte nodded to him, then started back down the driveway to the car.

"Can you believe that?" Ally frowned as she settled into the passenger seat. "Around Ricco, Nola was this sweet and caring woman, but at home she would throw things?"

"I'm not sure." Charlotte sighed as she started the car. "Sometimes people exaggerate things. But I don't see why a neighbor would lie about all of the fighting. I think there was definitely more to Ronaldo and Nola's marriage than we first realized. Let's see what he has to say." She drove the short distance to the bar.

"Wow, this place does look pretty shady." Ally winced as Charlotte put the car in park and stared through the windshield at the tiny rectangular building. She only counted two visible windows. The door appeared narrow and made of solid wood. "Not many cars in the parking lot, either."

"Perfect, that just means that it will be easy to

spot him." Charlotte opened the car door and stepped out. "Let's go, no time to waste."

Ally stared after her grandmother as she strode across the dirt and gravel parking lot, straight toward the door. It always amazed her that Charlotte seemed to have no fear. Despite her desire to be brave, Ally often thought she couldn't compare to her grandmother. As she followed after her, her heart pounded. What if the neighbor's warning had been accurate? Were they walking into a dangerous place?

"Ally, it's alright, we're together." Charlotte wrapped her arm around Ally's then pushed the door open.

CHAPTER 15

The interior of the bar had a heavy scent, a mixture of smoke and sweat. The dim lighting made the ambience even more bleak. A handful of men sat at the bar, with an empty stool between each of them. Only one small table was occupied, Ally recognized the man slumped forward across the table right away.

"Ronaldo." She walked up to the table without the slightest hesitation. "What are you doing here?"

"What does it look like?" Ronaldo slurred his words as he lifted his head off of his folded arms. "What are you doing here?"

"We're checking on you." Charlotte pulled a chair up to the other side of him and sat down in it. "It looks like it's a good thing we are. How do you plan to get home? Crawl?"

"What do you care?" Ronaldo grabbed his beer and took a swig. "You're the ones who took my father from me!"

"To make sure he was safe." Ally looked into his eyes. "The way you two were fighting, it was bound to get worse. Did you get so angry before you were with Nola, or only after?"

"Nola, Nola, Nola." Ronaldo's head sank down into his hands as he repeated her name. "Why did she have to die? Now, everything is a mess!"

"You must really miss her." Charlotte lowered her voice. "Just because you weren't together, doesn't mean you shouldn't grieve for her."

"Grieve for her?" Ronaldo rolled his eyes. "I won't be shedding a single tear for that woman. I thought I had finally found the one. When we first met, it was like my whole world had turned upside down. She was so sweet, so kind. She didn't give me a hard time about my bad habits. I thought she was perfect."

"And then?" Ally met his eyes, though they roamed and refused to focus.

"It was little things at first. I'd find out that she told my father that I said something I never said. I'd question her, and she'd insist that maybe my father was getting a little confused. Then it started to escalate. Each time I confronted her about it she told me I was the crazy one. Then she stopped being kind. She started being harsh. I'd demand to know why she was lying to my father about me, and she'd end up throwing things at me and threatening me. Of course my father didn't believe me. He believed her instead." Ronaldo's hand tightened around his beer, to the point that he began to crush the can. "She turned him against me, and I just stood by and let it happen!"

"That must have been infuriating." Ally pointed to the can before he could completely crush it. "Ronaldo, it wasn't right for her to treat you like that."

"No, it wasn't." Ronaldo's hand relaxed as he did his best to look straight at Ally. "But she's gone now. The worst thing is that I can't prove to my father that she was lying to him about me. He'll never believe me." He took the last swig of beer from the crumpled can then shook his head. "I still don't know why she did what she did. Or why I still miss her." With one sharp jerk of his hand he finished crushing the can, then tossed it on the floor. "She ruined my life, and I still miss her."

Ronaldo stood up from the table, wobbled a little to the right, then leaned on his chair to steady himself.

"Ronaldo, let me help you." Ally stood up and reached for his elbow to steady him.

"No." Ronaldo jerked his arm away. "No more help. I'm not taking any more help from anyone." He stumbled toward the door.

"Let me get you a cab." The bartender came around the bar and followed after Ronaldo.

"Ally don't." Charlotte caught her hand before she could follow them. "Let him go. He has said all he's going to say, and he may be unpredictable when he's drunk. At least we know he won't be driving home."

~

"I know that Ronaldo is a good suspect." Ally glanced at her grandmother as she drove back toward the shop. "So, why do I feel so terrible for him?"

"If what he's saying is true, if Nola did treat him so terribly, then it's only natural to feel that way, Ally. But you have to remember, we're only hearing one side of the story. Nola can't tell us hers."

"You're right, and the majority of people who

knew her, loved her, or at least thought that she was a kind person." Ally rested her head against the window. "I just can't shake the way Ronaldo spoke about her. He insists that he doesn't care that she's dead, then confesses to missing her. He just seems so conflicted."

"He does." Charlotte pulled into the parking lot of the chocolate shop. "But that doesn't mean that he couldn't have been so conflicted that he snapped and decided to get rid of what he viewed as the problem."

"True. But we also can't rule out Barnaby just yet." Ally stepped out of the car. "I think I'll make a few batches of caramels. I have some, but they are so popular this time of year I want to make sure we have extra."

"I'll help you." Charlotte followed her to the door.

"Mee-Maw, it's okay, I can do it." Ally fumbled for the keys.

"I'm here to help, sweetheart." Charlotte slid her own key into the lock. "I know that you're trying to do everything yourself, but there's nothing wrong with a little help."

"Thanks." Ally smiled as she followed her grandmother into the shop. "I appreciate the help, but I really love the company."

Ally turned on some music and the two of them

danced to it as they melted chocolate, boiled sugar and dipped the candies. She hadn't felt this relaxed in days and actually forgot about the murder for a few minutes.

Just after Ally finished setting the candies on the tray to harden, she heard a light knock on the front door.

"Who could that be?" She frowned as she looked toward the door.

"Mrs. Bing?" Charlotte raised an eyebrow.

"It's a bit late for her." Ally stepped out of the kitchen.

"I don't think there will ever be a time that is too late for chocolate, for Mrs. Bing." Charlotte laughed as she followed after her.

"It's Christian!" Ally smiled as the reporter waved at them through the front window. She grabbed the metal handle on the door and twisted the lock. A cool burst of air rushed through the door as she opened it. "Christian, what are you doing here?"

"I wanted to check on the progress of your sleuthing. I'm waiting for the big scoop, you know." Christian shivered as he tugged off his gloves. "It's getting really cold out there. We might get snow after all!"

"Christian, what about your investigating? Have

you found anything new?" Charlotte led him to the front counter and uncovered a dish of chocolate-covered nuts.

"Not really, I thought I'd be able to find you two here." Christian grinned as he grabbed a handful of chocolate-covered peanuts and tossed them in his mouth. "You always do your best thinking while making candy, don't you?"

"You know us too well." Ally grinned as she leaned against the counter. Her enthusiasm faded as she shook her head. "Unfortunately, it doesn't seem to be working too well for us tonight. We're convinced we have at least two good suspects, but we just can't seem to connect the final dots we need."

"Oh? Who is your main suspect?" Christian accepted a cup of coffee from Charlotte. "Thank you so much. I've been looking forward to this all day."

"Right now we're focusing on Ronaldo. He had a very strong motive, plus he was at Freely Lakes not long after the murder took place." Ally turned to refill the coffee pot, only to find her grandmother already in the process. She turned back to Christian. "The problem is, we can't figure out how he got in and out of the common room without being seen. He has quite a temper, and yet no one heard him in an argument with Nola. It's possible that he planned the murder and carried it out as quietly as possible, but if he did, how did he know that Nola was in the common room?"

"Maybe Ricco told him?" Charlotte rested her elbows on the counter and tipped her head back and forth. "We've been focused on the murderer either being Ronaldo or Ricco, but what if they were working together?"

"Ricco?" Christian smiled. "Now, there's an interesting suspect. I can see what you mean about those dots. Ronaldo is a good suspect, sure, but don't you think it's too obvious?"

"What do you mean?" Charlotte narrowed her eyes. "It's pretty common for a spouse or ex-spouse to be the guilty party when someone is murdered. So, why shouldn't we focus on the obvious suspect?"

"I'm not saying you shouldn't." Christian shrugged. "But look at it this way. If Ronaldo wanted Nola dead, why would he murder her at Freely Lakes? I'm sure he had a good idea of her routine. Why not follow her and carry out the deed in a less visible place?"

"That's a good point." Charlotte pursed her lips. "I hadn't considered that. It doesn't make sense for him to plan to murder Nola at Freely Lakes. But it didn't look like the murder was premeditated."

"Okay, let's try to clear our heads." Ally took a deep breath of the coffee and chocolate laced air. "Let's let go of Ronaldo for a second, and consider our other options. Well, there's still Janene. As far as we know, Ricco is too weak to have wielded the murder weapon. Who else do we have?"

"The thief." Charlotte nodded. "Whoever that might be. Possibly, Barnaby. We know that he has a picture of Nola on his phone. Maybe he was following her for some reason."

"A picture?" Christian's eyes widened. "What picture?"

"This." Ally pulled up the photograph on her phone. "I snapped a picture of it, it was on Barnaby's phone. It seems pretty clear that she didn't know the photograph was being taken. That's weird."

"It is." Christian studied the photo. "Do you mind if I take a closer look?"

"Feel free." Ally handed the phone to him. "I'm not sure what you're hoping to find, though."

"This." Christian expanded the picture, then moved it up to show Ally some text at the bottom of it. "You took a photo of this from his text messages, so he sent this picture to someone. I can see the phone number he sent it to. He might have taken the picture, but it might not have been for him, if he then decided to send it to someone else."

"I did take a snap of it from his messages, but I didn't realize the number he sent it to was there." Ally gasped as she looked up at him. "Clever thinking."

"Reporters do have to do a bit of sleuthing, too, you know." Christian smiled. "Let's call it."

"Good idea!" Ally took the phone from him. She entered the number into her phone. She held her breath as it began to ring. By the sixth ring, she'd lost hope that anyone would answer, but she thought the voicemail might still tell her something. "Mailbox is full." She frowned as she ended the call. "It didn't say who the number belonged to."

"A bit of a dead end for now." Christian shook his head. "Sorry I couldn't help more. But I will look into it more."

"You've been a huge help." Charlotte handed him a box of candy. "You gave us a new lead to look into. It might be too late for the person to pick up. We'll try again in the morning."

"Good plan." Christian took the candy and grinned. "I'll see what else I can dig up, so I can earn more of these treats."

As Christian walked out the door, Ally turned her

attention to her grandmother. "Who do you think Barnaby sent the picture to?"

"I'm not sure, but hopefully tomorrow will bring us some more information." Charlotte hugged her. "Once those candies are put away, we both need to go home and get some rest."

CHAPTER 16

*A*lly awoke to a furry tail sprawled across her face. The orange fuzz tickled her nostrils as she took a breath.

"Peaches!" She pulled the cat away from her face and snuggled her against her chest instead. "What have I told you about sleeping on my face?" She grinned as the cat nuzzled her cheeks. "Such a sweetie." She took a few minutes to pet her, then sat up in bed. She saw a snout resting on the end of the bed and two large, eager eyes. "Morning Arnold." She laughed as she got up and gave the pig a cuddle.

Ally had been up later than she intended, going over the possibilities in the case. She'd finally fallen asleep hoping that the morning would bring some clarity, but as she padded into the kitchen, followed by a meowing cat and a snorting pig, she didn't feel any more confident about the investigation.

"Who did he send that picture to, Peaches?" Ally added some food to her dish and set it down on the floor for her to eat.

Arnold nudged past Ally's hand with his snout as she filled his bowl.

"Easy now, there's plenty." Ally laughed as she gave his head a light pat.

She started a pot of coffee, then showered and dressed. She let Arnold and Peaches into the backyard to play. As she poured herself a cup, she heard Arnold squeal with happiness, then the back door swung open wider.

"Ally?"

"Oh, did you smell the coffee from the station?" Ally grinned as she poured another mug and offered it to Luke. "Wow, you are a sight for sore eyes."

"I was just thinking the same thing." Luke took the mug and leaned against the counter beside her as he looked into her eyes. "I have missed you so much."

"Me too. It sounded like Arnold did, too." Ally placed a light kiss on his lips. "I'm so glad you had a few minutes to stop by."

"Really, just a few." Luke sighed as he chased after her for one more kiss. "I've already been out to

Freely and back this morning, hoping that I'd cracked the case."

"Oh? What were you doing out there?" Ally sipped her coffee.

"Just following up on a few things. I went to see if Barnaby's brother, Scott, knew where he was. I still want to speak to Barnaby again and I had hoped I would get some information from Scott, but he turned me away at the door. He insisted he had no idea where Barnaby could be." Luke set his mug down. "I got the feeling that he wasn't telling me the whole truth, but the more I pushed the more he resisted. If I can get enough cause, I might be able to get a search warrant to see if Barnaby is hiding somewhere on the property. But it's going to take more than I have at the moment. Which is why I only have a moment." He gave her another quick kiss. "Thanks for the coffee, sweetheart."

"Thanks for the moment." Ally looked into his eyes, then took a breath. "I can't believe I'm going to get to call you husband soon."

"Thank you for that reminder." Luke grinned as he headed for the door. "Thinking of you in your wedding dress is a perfect way to get through this day!"

Ally's cheeks warmed as her heart pounded.

Husband? Wedding dress? The thoughts made her head spin. Prior to Nola's death, planning the wedding had been top priority, now it felt like a guilty indulgence.

Ally made sure that Peaches and Arnold had everything they needed, then gave them each a pat and said goodbye. As she got into her car, her phone rang. She saw it was Christian and quickly answered.

"Christian."

"Hey Ally." Christian sounded full of energy. "I followed up on that number. It turns out, it belongs to Barnaby's brother, Scott."

"It does?" Ally looked through the windshield. "Why would he send a photo of Nola to his brother?"

"No idea. I tried the number again but no one answered."

"I'm going to Freely Lakes now but can you text me his brother's address. I want to go out there to see if I can find him."

"Sure. I have a few things to do but I can come with you later if you want?"

"No, that's ok. I want to go as soon as possible. I'll take my grandmother with me." Ally started the car. "If I find out anything I'll let you know."

"I'll do the same." Christian ended the call.

On her way to Freely Lakes, Ally ran through all of the possibilities in her mind. If Barnaby had sent a picture of Nola to his brother, there had to be a reason. Could the brother have been in on the murder? Maybe Barnaby asked him to commit the crime, while he was otherwise occupied, so that he would have an alibi. But the murder didn't appear to be premeditated. So, what were the two brothers up to, and how was Nola caught in the middle of it?

"Good morning, Ally." Charlotte greeted her at the door. "I was surprised to see you text so early."

"I wanted to get an early start because I want to take a drive out to Barnaby's brother's house." Ally filled her in on Christian's discovery, and Luke's visit to Barnaby's brother. "I thought maybe if we took a look around, or spoke to him, we might be able to find something."

"That sounds great to me. Barnaby had to have a reason to send that picture to his brother." Charlotte settled into the passenger seat. "Did you get any sleep last night?"

"Some." Ally smiled. "I'm feeling energized now that I had a few minutes with Luke. I had honestly almost forgotten about the wedding."

"We can't forget that." Charlotte patted her hand. "I'm very excited for you, Ally."

"Thanks, Mee-Maw." Ally flashed her a smile, then sighed. "But I'd feel a lot better if we had this solved." She drove toward the address that Christian had given her. As she turned onto the street, she narrowed her eyes. "We're looking for number fifty-two."

"It's that house on the left." Charlotte pointed through the windshield at a small, beige house set back from the road and surrounded by well-tended, tall bushes. But what really caught her attention were the Christmas decorations. They were everywhere. There was everything from an inflatable Santa coming out of the chimney to his sleigh and reindeer in the front yard.

"Wow, you can't exactly miss it." Ally smiled at the sight of the large decorations.

"No, you can't." Charlotte pointed off to the side, in the driveway where a blue car was parked. "Great, it looks like he's home."

Ally knocked on the door, then stepped back as she waited for it to open.

"I don't think he's going to answer." Charlotte crossed her arms as she stared at the window not far from the door. "I just saw him peek out and walk away."

"I'll try one more time." Ally knocked again, much harder.

"Nothing." Charlotte shook her head. "If he refused to talk to Luke, then he likely doesn't want to talk to two strangers either."

As they turned to walk away, a woman walked up the driveway with a toddler in her arms. Ally noticed a small SUV parked behind their car along the road. She guessed that someone who lived in the house would have used the driveway.

"Excuse me, ma'am, do you know if anyone is home here?" Ally met her eyes.

"Sure, my brother is here." She frowned. "Who are you?"

"We're looking for Barnaby." Charlotte smiled. "Do you know where he might be?"

"You're looking for my brother Barnaby?" She shifted the toddler from one hip to the other. "Why?"

"He seems to have gone missing, and we're a little concerned." Charlotte held up her phone with a picture of Nola on it. "Do you know this woman?"

"Her?" She glared at the phone. "Oh yes, of course I know her!"

"How do you know her?" Ally's heart began to race.

"She almost married my oldest brother, Scott." She tipped her head toward the house. "She was living here with him, when our mom got sick. She would tend to her every need, and seemed to enjoy spending time with her. They had begun to plan the wedding, when she changed. Our mother was getting sicker, and we were all worried about her. But she started acting like it was our fault somehow. Soon, our mother refused to see us. She cut us out of her life, out of her will." She blinked back a few tears. "It was a terrible time for us. I am so glad she is out of our lives."

"You're glad she's dead?" Ally narrowed her eyes.

"What?" The woman held her daughter tighter against her body. "What are you talking about?"

"She's been murdered." Charlotte raised her eyebrows. "You haven't heard?"

"I've been out of town. I just got back." She shook her head as her cheeks reddened. "Look, I don't know where my brother is, and I'm sorry that someone killed her, but honestly, she hasn't been part of our lives in years. There's no reason my brother would be involved with her."

"Barnaby was involved with her." Charlotte couldn't let her know that they had looked at Barnaby's phone and seen that he had sent a photograph of Nola to her other brother. "He worked at the same place where she was when she died."

"Barnaby didn't even know Ana. He never met her. He just saw pictures of her. He wasn't living in the area at the time when our mother got sick and didn't make it back in time before she died." She sighed. "Look, I don't want to talk about this anymore. Whatever you think Barnaby did, he didn't. Whoever killed her, well, maybe she was as terrible to them as she was to us." She turned and hurried up the driveway.

Ally met Charlotte's eyes and sighed. "It sounds like a very familiar story, doesn't it?"

"It does. Maybe that's why she changed her name, to leave the past behind."

"Maybe." Ally looked at the time. "I have to open the shop."

"I'll come with you, that way we can get on top of the orders and then I think it's time we speak to Albert again." Charlotte nodded.

"Okay, thanks Mee-Maw." Ally headed toward the chocolate shop.

They were busy from the moment they opened the front door and they barely had two seconds break, but Ally loved every second of working in the shop with her grandmother and serving eager customers delicious treats. Her grandmother always surprised her with how much energy she had. They didn't even have time to catch up with Mrs. Bing, Mrs. Cale and Mrs. White when they came into the shop. Although, the three ladies didn't seem to mind as they made their way through the sample tray.

"I can't believe it's time to close already." Ally sighed as she looked at her watch.

"I know, that was full on, but fun." Charlotte smiled as she wiped down the counter.

"Let's get this place cleaned up and then go see Albert."

"I am going to take some chocolates for the residents." Charlotte gestured to a couple of boxes of chocolates. "I think it might cheer them up."

"Can't ever have enough chocolate." Ally smiled.

After closing up the shop, Ally and Charlotte settled in the car.

"What's our plan?" Ally started the car and headed toward Freely Lakes.

"I want to speak to Albert first. There was something going on between him and Barnaby when they had that argument we overheard. My guess is that Albert knows more than he's revealing. He may not have known about the murder, but he might just know more about the thefts than he claimed. Maybe we can shake something out of him about where Barnaby might be hiding." Charlotte smiled. "He might have a stronger reason to kill Nola. It may not just be about her getting him into trouble and him possibly getting fired. It may have to do with the way she treated his brother."

"I think you're right." Ally turned onto the street that led to Freely Lakes. "Add to that the fact that he can't be found, and we can be fairly certain that Barnaby is the killer. Since he had never met Nola, he likely sent the picture to his brother to confirm her identity. Once he did, maybe Barnaby decided to confront her. Maybe things got heated, and he killed her."

"It makes sense." Charlotte nodded. "He probably also knew about the tension between Ronaldo and Nola, and might have hoped that Ronaldo would get blamed for the murder."

"Now, all we have to do is find him." Ally parked at the entrance closest to the manager's office. "Let's make sure that Albert tells us what he knows." She led the way down the hallway to the office.

Charlotte peeked past her as she stepped into the office. Albert had the phone pressed to his ear. His face was flushed, and beads of sweat dotted his forehead.

The moment he saw them, he put down the phone.

"I'm just leaving, ladies, sorry." Albert quickly shut his laptop and pushed past them out of the office.

"Just a second, Albert, we need to speak with you, please." Ally followed after him.

Charlotte matched their pace. "It's important, Albert."

"I really don't have time to talk." Albert sighed as they followed him down the hall. "You have no idea how many fires I'm trying to put out today."

"I can only imagine." Charlotte quickened her steps to catch up with him. "But we only have a few questions for you about Barnaby. You hired him, I would assume that you would know the most about him."

"I didn't hire him, I inherited him." Albert slid his key into the lock on the doorknob of his apartment. "Barnaby was working here when I became the manager." He started to push open the door. "If it had been up to me, he wouldn't have been hired. But he was already so familiar with the way things worked around here, and so many of the people that lived here, I couldn't dismiss him."

"You were that unhappy with his work that you

considered letting him go?" Ally stepped forward just as he stepped into his apartment. She casually positioned her foot between the door and the frame. "Do you have any idea where he might be?"

"Barnaby acted more like the manager than a maintenance man. I have never enjoyed that about him. He walks around here like he's in charge of everything." Albert frowned as he looked down at her foot. "Like I said, I'm terribly busy. I have a meeting, I just need to get something from my apartment first."

"Please." Ally looked into his eyes. "All we need is two minutes of your time, then we'll be out of your hair. It must have been such a struggle to take over as a new manager here with Barnaby acting that way."

"It wasn't easy." Albert took a step back from the door. "It took time, but we did adjust to each other. He became more compliant, and I became more flexible. Perhaps, that was a mistake on my part." He shook his head as he dropped his keys in a dish on a table beside the door, then walked toward the living room.

Ally followed after him. "You said that he was letting people keep cats without you knowing about it, right? Who in particular? If he was close with them, maybe one of them will have an idea of where he might be."

"I'm not sure." Albert shrugged. "That wasn't the only way he shirked the rules around here. We have a strict policy about delivery services, yet he'd always wave them through the door without checking their identification or verifying their delivery. He didn't take the need for security very seriously."

"And yet you never suspected him of the thefts that have been occurring?" Charlotte narrowed her eyes.

"What?" Albert stared at her for a long moment.

"The thefts. It's pretty clear that he would have easy access to the apartments. So, why didn't you ever suspect him?"

"Barnaby may be a lot of things, but he isn't a thief." Albert shook his head. "At least, I didn't think he was. Now, I don't know what to think." He walked over to a small office and stepped through the door. He closed the door halfway. "You really have to go now, I have so much to do."

Charlotte noticed a cat statue positioned beside the computer. Her heart skipped a beat as it stood out to her. He'd claimed he hated cats. So, why did he have a statue of one? She placed her hand on the door to push it open a little farther.

"Okay, it's time for you both to leave." Albert grabbed the knob of the door and pulled it shut as he met her eyes. "I gave you your two minutes, I don't have another second to spare."

"Albert, just one more question!" Ally called out just as the door snapped shut.

"Let's go." Charlotte grabbed Ally's arm and tugged her out of the apartment.

"Mee-Maw, what is it?" Ally met her eyes.

"Something isn't right about any of this." Charlotte shook her head. "I want to speak to Ricco again." She led Ally toward Ricco's apartment. She wanted to tell her about the cat statue, but she wanted to speak to Ricco first, and she didn't want to discuss the statue when there were residents in the hallway. She wanted to see what Ricco had to say about his last interactions with Barnaby. Maybe Barnaby tried to warn him about Nola. If so, that puts him and Ronaldo right back in the center of all of this.

Ally knocked on the door of Ricco's apartment. After a long moment, Ricco opened the door.

"Charlotte." Ricco nodded cheerfully. "Come in."

"How are you holding up?" Charlotte asked.

"Good, thank you." Ricco smiled. "I feel like I have a lot more energy. But I am missing Nola, of course." He nodded. "I've been trying to keep up with what Nola told me to take, but there are so many pills and vitamins, I just can't keep them all straight."

"We're sorry to bother you." Charlotte sat down beside him and patted his arm. "Would you like me to call the nurse for you? She can come check things out?" Freely Lakes had a nurse that was available to the residents if needed.

"She's already been here this morning. She said that everything looked fine, but she didn't think I should be alone. I told her that I'll be fine." Ricco nodded. "I don't mind being alone. Like I said I am feeling quite strong today."

"That's good. What about Barnaby?" Ally smiled. "He helps you out sometimes, right? Have you seen him?"

"Oh yes, Barnaby." Ricco nodded. "I haven't been able to reach him."

"Did Barnaby have anything to say about Nola?" Ally raised an eyebrow. "Did he ever mention knowing her from before?"

"Knowing her?" Ricco shook his head. "No, but Nola insisted that I could trust him. She made me change the lock on my door, and give only him the key."

"Why was that?" Charlotte looked into his eyes.

"She said he was the only one that could be trusted with it." Ricco shrugged. "I just did as she said."

"Who else normally has a key for the apartment?" Charlotte's eyes widened as she began to piece things together.

"Albert, the manager. But she made me promise not to tell him about changing the locks." Ricco sighed. "I don't know why."

"Call me if you need anything." Charlotte stood up and headed for the door with Ally close behind her.

CHAPTER 17

*A*lly barely had a chance to catch her breath as Charlotte hurried her down the hall.

"Mee-Maw, what's going on?" Ally noticed the tightness of her grip.

"Not here." Charlotte tugged her back toward her apartment. Once she pulled her inside, she closed the door, and turned to face her. "I think we've found our thief, and our murderer."

"What?" Ally's eyes widened. "Are you talking about Barnaby?"

"No, I'm not. I'm talking about Albert." Charlotte pointed to the door. "He's been fooling us this whole time. Nola was on to the thief, that's why she was asking so many questions of everyone. We thought that she had figured out it was

Barnaby, but she didn't. She figured out it was Albert!"

"Albert?" Ally shook her head. "But why would he steal from the residents?"

"My guess is he's facing some serious financial struggles. Whatever the reason, he had the keys to all of the apartments, and a perfect excuse if anyone caught him, as he could claim he was conducting an inspection." Charlotte frowned.

"Okay, but what proof do we have?" Ally sighed. "We can't just accuse him without it."

"The cat statue. I saw it inside his apartment. I'm certain it's the one stolen from Daniel. Which means he's the one that stole it. The problem is, I think he noticed me noticing it, now all he has to do is get rid of it, and our accusation will mean nothing." Charlotte took a sharp breath. "If only I'd had a chance to take a picture of it, we could get Daniel to confirm it, but he hurried us out of there so fast."

"So, you think that Nola discovered Albert was the thief and that was why she replaced the lock on Ricco's door and made sure that only Barnaby had the key? Why would she do that? Wouldn't she have known that Barnaby was her ex's brother?" Ally began to pace back and forth. "She wouldn't have trusted him if she had known that."

"She didn't know. She'd never met him. Barnaby had likely seen pictures of her, but there's a good chance she didn't see pictures of him, at least not recent ones. So, she likely didn't recognize his face. Barnaby suspected who she was and sent a photo to his brother to confirm. But she had no idea." Charlotte pursed her lips. "We've been hunting the wrong guy."

"That might be why he disappeared. If he knew about Nola's history with his family, then he likely expected to be the main suspect once the police figured out the connection. So, he took off to protect himself." Ally snapped her fingers. "Yes, that all fits!"

"Except, maybe he didn't take off." Charlotte bit into her bottom lip. "Maybe, he figured out it was Albert, and Albert had to get rid of him, too."

"Oh no." Ally stopped short and stared at her grandmother. "You think he might have killed him, too?"

"I think there's a good chance." Charlotte shivered. "I'd rather not believe it, but that's how it's adding up."

"But we still have no proof." Ally sank down in one of Charlotte's overstuffed chairs. "Without some kind of evidence it won't make any difference."

"Luke can at least take him in for questioning,

can't he?" Charlotte sat down across from her. "It would be a start."

"It would be, but Luke might not. If he did, he would only end up having to release him, unless he can get him to confess." Ally shook her head as she sat forward in the chair. "If he's smart enough to steal, and murder, do you really think he's going to confess?"

"Probably not without a lot of persuasion." Charlotte leaned forward. "No, we need a better plan. We need some way to force him to expose himself."

"Like a trap?" A smile flashed across Ally's lips. "Mee-Maw, that's a fantastic idea. That's exactly what we need to do."

"But how?" Charlotte met her eyes. "Any thoughts?"

"We believe that Albert has been stealing from the apartments, right?" Ally stood up and walked over to the shelves beside her grandmother's television set. She looked at the small figurines lined up on each one as well as photos of Arnold and Peaches. They immediately brought a smile to her face. "He's stolen from multiple apartments in Freely Lakes. That isn't just about stealing, that's about compulsion. If he's done it that many times, then I'd bet he'd be unable to resist doing it again."

"That's a brilliant idea, Ally. All we need to do is come up with some bait that he would want." Charlotte stood up and walked over to a tall cabinet with glass doors in the dining room. "I have just the thing."

"What is it?" Ally followed her over to the cabinet.

"Your grandmother's silver. It's been passed down through our family for generations. It's really not worth that much, but Albert doesn't know that. I'll start some chatter about having it appraised for a very high amount. Then, we'll sweeten the story by letting everyone know that I'm going to help you at the shop and I'll be staying at your place tonight." Charlotte set the box of silver on the dining room table.

"I'm sure he'll break in to try to get it." Ally nodded. "We can be here and catch him in the act."

"No." Charlotte shook her head. "No way, that's too risky."

"What?" Ally frowned. "But it was your idea."

"Yes, I want to set a trap for him, but we don't need to be here to do that. If we're right, and he's the murderer, he might decide to get rid of us, too. I have that tracker I was going to give you for Peaches. We can put it in the silverware. When he steals it, the tracker will trace it to his place. We can do all of this while you and I are safe at the shop. When the item is on the move, we'll let Luke know and he can swoop in, catch him in the act and make the arrest." Charlotte smiled. "What do you think?"

"I think that's the perfect plan." Ally gazed at her as she shook her head. "You are amazing, Mee-Maw."

"We'll see." Charlotte winked. "Let's get to work, there isn't a moment to lose. I'll make sure that Mrs. Bing, Mrs. Cale, and Mrs. White know all about this silver, and I'll ask them to spread it around to as many people as they can. I'll also mention that we'll be at the shop busy with Christmas orders, and that I plan to spend the night at your house. That way Albert will be very tempted. He was so nervous today. He's stolen so many things that I guess he could use the money."

"Great thinking, Mee-Maw. I'll give Luke a heads up so that when we text him, he'll be expecting it." As Charlotte called Mrs. Bing, Ally sent Luke a detailed text. Hopefully, by the next morning, the murderer would be caught, Christmas would be saved, and the wedding plans could begin again.

*L*ater that evening, Ally piled Peaches and Arnold into her car and headed for the chocolate shop. Even though she had no reason to believe her grandmother and her would be in any danger, she always felt safer with her pets close to her. It was also a nice outing for them and she had barely seen them all day. She parked beside Jeff's car, then led the animals toward the courtyard. She let them off their leashes. Peaches gave a quiet hiss as she looked toward the large bushes in the corner. "What is it?" Ally frowned. "Did another cat get in here?" As she crouched down to pet Peaches she smiled at the cat's soft meow.

"It's okay, Peaches. I know you can tell that something is wrong. I'm a little tense, huh?" Ally laughed as the cat's tail swept across her cheek. "But everything's going to be fine, I promise. We're going to catch the bad guy, and by tomorrow everything will be a little bit better." She frowned as she thought about Nola. "I only wish I could say the same for Nola and Barnaby. Whatever happened between them in the past, now they've likely suffered the same fate. If only we had figured this out sooner, we might have been able to protect Barnaby."

Ally held her breath as the bushes rustled. Seconds later Arnold burst forth with a snort and headed straight for them. "Playing hide and seek I see, Arnold!" Ally laughed as she wrapped her arms around the pig's neck and placed a kiss on the top of his head. "You gave us a little scare, you silly pig."

"What's all the commotion out here?" Charlotte poked her head out through the door to the courtyard. "Oh, I see you brought the kids!"

"That's okay, I hope." Ally stood up as Charlotte greeted Arnold. "I just feel better with them here."

"Of course, it is. I have a feeling we may need the entertainment. It may be hours before Albert takes the bait. If he even takes the bait."

"Great, because I have a huge order of Yule logs to make." Ally grinned as she walked toward her grandmother. "Remember how you said I should ask for your help?"

"Happy to do it." Charlotte ducked back inside the shop.

Ally followed after her. She glanced back at Peaches just as the cat prowled toward the bushes again.

"Be nice to Arnold, Peaches! No scratching!"

Peaches flicked her tail.

Ally pulled the door shut, then walked over to the sink to wash up.

"You already have the computer set up?"

"Yes, I put it right here, so we'd be able to easily see it all night. But Christian helped me set up a notification to alert us if there is any movement of the tag. Of course, in exchange, I had to promise him the story and a Yule log." Charlotte shrugged. "It seemed like an even exchange."

"It does." Ally gazed at the screen. "Do you really think Albert will break in?"

"I think there's a very good chance." Charlotte walked over to one of the long, stainless steel counters affixed to the back wall of the kitchen. "I've gotten started on the Yule logs, the cakes will need to be rolled up soon."

"Great, thanks so much." Ally pulled on her

apron, then settled into the process of rolling the cakes. The heat of the moist cake emanated through the towel she rolled it in. The process soon eased her into a relaxed state. The delicious aromas that filled the kitchen brought a faint smile to her lips. Her grandmother's excited chatter about the wedding made her laugh. "Mee-Maw, there's no way we're having doves."

"Goats then?" Charlotte smiled as she glanced over at her. "Just a few, nothing outlandish."

"Goats?" Ally laughed again. "What in the world would we do with goats?"

"Oh, it's a new trend. You dress them up like the wedding party, and they go down the aisle first! Oh, it's so adorable!"

"No way, I think a cat and a pig will be enough animals at my wedding." Ally grinned.

A sharp beep emitted from the computer.

"Ally! The silverware is on the move!" Charlotte tugged her over to the computer.

"I don't see it." Ally stared at the screen. "Maybe it's a false alarm?"

"Look!" Charlotte pointed to the red dot that appeared on the map. "It's on the move!"

"I'll call Luke right now." Ally pulled out her phone.

"No, not yet." Charlotte put her hand on Ally's shoulder. "Not yet, let's make sure it leaves the apartment first."

"Where else would it go?" Ally frowned.

The dot started moving down the hall.

"It's on the move for sure." Charlotte nodded. "Call him!"

Ally placed the call. "Ugh, I got his voicemail. I'll text him." She fired off a quick text. As she hit send, she heard Peaches yowl from behind the shop. "Oh, what is that cat up to?"

"Not now, Ally, we have to keep an eye on the silverware!" Charlotte clicked a button which made the map expand across the whole screen.

Ally's phone beeped.

"It's from Luke, he has caught Albert in the act."

"Good." Charlotte smiled. "I can't believe it! Stealing from his own tenants!"

"How terrible!" Ally took a sharp breath. "Oh, Mee-Maw, this means that he probably did do something horrible to Barnaby. That poor man, and his family, they've already been through so much."

"I know." Charlotte sighed, then shook her head. "Luke must have arrested Albert. Ally?"

Ally froze as she felt the blade against her back. She didn't dare to take a breath, let alone speak. The hand that held her arm tightened until pain coursed from her fingertips to her shoulder.

"Ally?" Charlotte turned toward her, then gasped. "Let her go, Barnaby!"

"Not a chance." Barnaby pressed the blade a little harder against Ally's back. "Step away from the computer and toss your phone on the floor. Now!"

Ally shivered with fear as she realized they had made a terrible mistake. Perhaps they had caught the thief red-handed, but they hadn't caught the murderer. At least not in the way they had intended.

"Barnaby, please." Ally's voice trembled. "You don't have to do this."

"It's too late for that now, Ally, far too late." Barnaby grabbed her arm.

Tears stung Ally's eyes as she glanced down at her phone. It was a new text from Luke. It was a thumbs up emoji. He had no idea they were in trouble. He believed he had caught the murderer.

CHAPTER 19

Charlotte's heart slammed against her chest. She could barely breathe past the panic that throbbed through her body as she saw the knife against Ally's back.

"Barnaby." Ally tossed her phone to the floor as he instructed and stepped away from the computer. "Whatever is going on here, it can stop right now. It doesn't have to go further than this. Albert is being arrested as we speak. We know he was the thief. Clearly, he killed Nola as well." Her mind spun as she realized that wasn't the truth. Barnaby was the killer. He had to be. Which meant he had a lot to lose.

"He didn't. He has an alibi." Barnaby narrowed his eyes. "He didn't want to admit to it, but he was with his bookie at the time, begging for his life because he was so far in debt. He'll tell the police that, if he's been caught. Then they'll know that it wasn't him." He frowned. "There is no way out of any of this, and you may not believe me, but none of this is my fault!"

"I do, I do believe you." Charlotte's eyes glazed with tears as she noticed Ally shift and twist against his grasp. A grimace flickered across her face. "Please Barnaby, you're hurting her."

"I'm doing what I have to do, what I've been forced to do." Barnaby drew a shaky breath. "I just need all of this to be over. This is the only way to make that happen."

"Tell me, Barnaby." Charlotte stared straight into his eyes. She hoped that if she bought a little time, she could come up with a way to escape. "Tell me the truth about what happened to your mother, and why Nola had to die because of it."

"My mother." Barnaby's chin trembled. "My mother was a beautiful woman. So innocent. So strong. When my sister told me how sick she was, I didn't believe it. She'd never been a sickly person. I called to speak to her doctors, and they all told me how they didn't understand what was happening. They couldn't seem to get her better, she was getting worse."

"Just like Ricco." Ally bit into her bottom lip as Barnaby jostled her.

"Yes, that's right. Nola wormed her way into my family, and then pushed everyone away from my mother. She convinced my mother that her family had turned against her. Her last moments were spent believing that she had lost all of us!" A sharp cry escaped his lips. "How can I live with that for the rest of my life?"

"What happened to your mother was terrible, Barnaby, but it doesn't make it okay to hurt us." Charlotte sighed as she took a step closer to him. "Nola had to be stopped, we understand that. She was manipulative, and she destroyed families."

"No!" Barnaby glared at her and shoved Ally away from himself far enough to reveal the knife he held. "She was a murderer! She was going to get away with it! She was the one who made my mother sick. First, she convinced her to change her will, then she poisoned her! I know she did! She disappeared before I could prove it and I couldn't find her. I thought there was nothing I could do about it."

"But then Nola came here." Ally tried to keep him talking.

"Yes, then I saw her with Ricco. When I went to his apartment to fix the light bulb, I saw the unlabeled medicine bottles. Just like the empty ones that I found in my mother's bedroom. Then I saw a picture of her in Ricco's room. She was wearing what looked like a necklace my mother used to have. I couldn't be sure that it was her, so I left in a rush to find out. She went by a different first name, but had the same features. Can you believe she had the nerve to come to me about Albert being the thief? She told me she needed me to keep him out of Ricco's apartment. She claimed she was trying to protect him, but I knew the truth." Barnaby sniffled, then shook his head. "I think she was worried that Albert would figure out she was poisoning Ricco and she wanted Albert out of the picture before he could prove it."

"You needed to make sure it was Ana." Ally's heart raced.

"I sent a picture of her to my brother and when he confirmed it was her, I nearly lost my mind. I confronted her. I wanted to protect Ricco, and I wanted her to own up to what she did."

"You should have gone to the police!" Charlotte gasped out her words. "What she did is unforgivable, Barnaby, but you can still go to the police now! Tell them what happened, and why you did what you did."

"I couldn't go to the police. I didn't have any proof. She told me as much. She promised me I would never be able to prove it, and Ricco would never believe me. She had him wrapped around her little finger, just like she'd had my mother! She said they were so stupid and desperate for love they didn't even know that she was killing them!" Barnaby shuddered. "I saw red. I never knew that was possible. But I saw it. I just grabbed the piece of wood, and I swung it at her head. I just wanted her to keep quiet! I just wanted her to pay for what she did! After I killed her, I made sure I emptied Ricco's unlabeled pill bottle so he wouldn't continue to be poisoned." He held the knife to Ally's throat and pulled her back against him. "I did what had to be done!"

"Yes! Barnaby, you did!" Charlotte shrieked as she saw Ally wince. "But you don't have to do this! Ally hasn't done anything to hurt you! Neither have I. Just let us go, Barnaby. The police will understand what happened. You're making things so much harder on yourself right now!"

"No, for once, I'm making them easier on myself." Barnaby relaxed his grasp some. His voice grew even and calm. "For once, I'm going to make things work out right. When I found out you two were asking my sister about me, I knew that you were on to me. I knew that you two had to die as well. Because I'm not going to spend the rest of my life in prison, I'm not going to let her win!"

"We didn't know," Charlotte whispered her words as she knew they didn't matter now.

A loud scratching at the back door startled Barnaby.

Charlotte reached for the arm that held the knife in the same moment that Ally lunged away from his grasp.

Arnold snorted and scratched at the back door again.

"No, you don't!" Barnaby shoved Charlotte to the ground. "You're manipulating me, too! I know it when I see it! If I had been there, I would have put a stop to all of it and protected my mother!"

Charlotte landed hard on the floor and winced in pain.

Barnaby grabbed onto Ally again.

"You're not going to get away with this! You're not going to ruin my life! I've had too much taken away already!"

The back door slammed open and Luke rushed through it with his gun drawn.

"Drop your weapon, Barnaby! Now!"

Stunned, Barnaby released the knife from his grasp, though he still held Ally tightly against him.

"You won't risk hurting her!"

"No, I won't." Luke stared straight at him. "But I'm not letting you leave with her either."

lly took a deep breath of the spices that wafted through the air. She listened to her grandmother's laughter as it drifted around the dining room. Though the two-bedroom cottage was small, it seemed perfectly cozy when filled with the warmth of friends and family. Mrs. Bing, Mrs. Cale, and Mrs. White sat around the table exchanging stories with Charlotte, as Ally carried the tray with a perfectly cooked turkey out of the kitchen.

"Let me get that for you." Luke took the tray from her hands as he smiled at her. "Peaches is perched and ready to attack." He tipped his head toward the bookshelf that Peaches perched on.

"Peaches!" Ally laughed. "You sneaky cat."

"Be nice." Luke set the tray down on the table.

"She's the hero, you know. If she hadn't decided to hunt me down, I might never have known how much danger you and Charlotte were in."

Everyone at the table quietened down and turned their attention to Luke.

"Tell us the story again, Luke." Mrs. Bing batted her eyes at him. "Please?"

"Didn't you read enough about it in the paper? I thought Christian's article was pretty good." Ally grinned.

"Luke tells it better!" Mrs. Cale whipped her napkin through the air, then settled it in her lap. "Just one more time, Luke."

"Alright, fine, if Ally doesn't mind." Luke met her eyes.

"I don't mind. I still can't believe it myself." Ally scooped the cat into her arms. "She really is my hero, and so is Arnold. If he hadn't scratched at the door, Barnaby might have decided to end things before you arrived." She looked at Luke. "But if it wasn't for you, Luke, Mee-Maw and I would not be here for Christmas this year. You are truly, one hundred percent, my hero."

"Aw, sweetheart." Luke pulled her close and kissed her. "I don't even want to think about that possibility, it breaks my heart."

"Don't." Ally gazed into his eyes. "We're all safe, and the wedding is on its way."

"I can't wait." Luke kissed her again.

"Okay, are we getting a story or a show?" Mrs. White threw a dinner roll at the two of them.

"Hey!" Ally laughed.

"There I was thinking that everything was fine. Albert was in custody, and he had concocted an outlandish story about being with his bookie at the time of the murder, but I didn't believe him. I tried to call Ally to check in with her, but she didn't answer. I thought maybe the call didn't go through, so I stepped outside. The moment I did, this little one—" Luke ran his fingers across the cat's fur. "Shredded my ankles. She wouldn't quit. She was yowling and hissing and spitting. I thought for sure she'd gone feral! When I tried to go back inside, she attacked me again. I tried to call Ally again, and still no answer." He took a slow breath, then shook his head. "That's when I knew. There was only one reason that Peaches would be acting that wild. She was scared. Then I was scared. I knew I had to get to Ally as fast as I could."

"She was right." Ally smiled as Peaches nuzzled her cheek. "She tried to warn me, too, before I went into the shop. She knew that Barnaby was in the bushes."

"To think that both of you, and Ricco, could be gone." Mrs. White shook her head, then took a sip of her wine. "It's still a tragedy that Nola was killed, but to find out that she was poisoning Ricco is shocking. What Barnaby did was wrong, but he very well might have saved Ricco's life."

"That's true, but let's try not to discuss it at dinner tonight." Ally let Peaches jump down from her arms. "When he and Ronaldo get here, I want to only talk about happy things."

"Like a goat in a tuxedo?" Charlotte grinned. "I can't think of anything happier!"

"What?" Luke raised an eyebrow. "Ally? Is this something new for the wedding?"

"No!" Ally laughed. "No, Mee-Maw! No goats!" She knew her grandmother was only joking.

As Ally settled at the table, the discussion shifted from goats, to flower arrangements, and special moments to look forward to during the ceremony. She reached across the table and took Luke's hand. As she gazed at him, the reflection from the candles on the table made his eyes sparkle. She'd known for a long time that he was the person she wanted to spend the rest of her life with, yet each time she looked into his eyes, she was surprised by just how lucky she was. She looked out the window at the snow that had begun to fall and felt even cozier. Maybe the Christmas season had gotten off to a rough start, but they had a lot to look forward to in the New Year. She couldn't wait to cherish every moment, starting with that moment.

Ally picked up her glass of wine and raised it into the air. "To creating happy memories, and valuing each moment we have with our loved ones!"

As everyone joined in on the toast, Ally felt Arnold and Peaches bump into her legs as they chased each other under the table.

The table shook. Luckily everyone had their glasses in the air.

"Yes, absolutely no goats." Ally laughed.

The End

INGREDIENTS:

Cake:

4 eggs, separated
3/4 cup superfine sugar
2 tablespoons milk
1/4 cup unsalted butter, melted
2 teaspoon vanilla extract
1/2 cup all-purpose flour
1/3 cup unsweetened cocoa powder, plus 1
tablespoon for dusting
1 teaspoon baking powder
1/4 teaspoon salt

Chocolate Cream Cheese Frosting:

8 ounces cream cheese, at room temperature
1 cup confectioners' sugar
3 ounces bittersweet chocolate, melted
1 teaspoon vanilla extract

Whipped Ganache Frosting:

6 ounces semisweet chocolate
6 ounces heavy cream

2 crushed candy canes for decorating if desired.

PREPARATION:

Preheat the oven to 350 degrees Fahrenheit. Grease a 17 x 12-inch jelly roll pan to hold the parchment paper in place. Line the pan with parchment paper, leaving some paper over the sides of the pan so the cake is easy to remove. Grease the parchment paper. We want the cake to come out of the pan very easily. Have a clean kitchen towel sprinkled with the tablespoon of cocoa powder ready for when the cake comes out of the oven.

For the cake:

Beat the egg yolks, sugar, milk, butter and vanilla extract together.

Mix together the all-purpose flour, unsweetened cocoa powder and baking powder.

Beat the egg whites and salt into stiff peaks.

Gradually add the dry ingredients to the egg yolk mixture.

Fold the beaten egg whites into the mixture a third at a time, being careful not to overmix. You want to keep as much of the air in the egg whites as possible.

Pour the batter into the pan. Place in the oven and bake for about 10 minutes. The cake is ready when it springs back when lightly pressed. Be careful not to overbake.

When the cake is ready, remove from the oven and invert onto the prepared kitchen towel. Remove the parchment paper. Roll up the cake with the towel starting from the narrow end.

Leave aside to cool completely. The cake can be cooled in the refrigerator.

For the chocolate cream cheese frosting:

Beat together the cream cheese and sugar. Add the melted chocolate and vanilla extract and beat until combined.

Unroll the cooled cake and spread a layer of the frosting over it.

Roll the cake up again without the towel.

For the whipped ganache frosting:

Break the chocolate into pieces in a heatproof bowl.

Gently heat the cream until it begins to steam. Remove from the heat before it boils.

Pour the cream over the chocolate and then leave for about 2 minutes so the chocolate begins to melt. Stir the mixture slowly until the chocolate has completely melted and is mixed with the cream.

Refrigerate for about 10 to 15 minutes. Whisk the frosting. Spread over the sides and top of the cake.

Sprinkle crushed candy canes over the top if desired.

225

Enjoy!!

LITTLE LEAF CREEK COZY MYSTERY SERIES

Chaos in Little Leaf Creek

Peril in Little Leaf Creek

Conflict in Little Leaf Creek

Action in Little Leaf Creek

CHOCOLATE CENTERED COZY MYSTERIES

The Sweet Smell of Murder

A Deadly Delicious Delivery

A Bitter Sweet Murder

A Treacherous Tasty Trail

Pastry and Peril

Trouble and Treats

Fudge Films and Felonies

Custom-Made Murder

Skydiving, Soufflés and Sabotage

Christmas Chocolates and Crimes

Hot Chocolate and Homicide

Chocolate Caramels and Conmen

Picnics, Pies and Lies

Devils Food Cake and Drama

Cinnamon and a Corpse

Cherries, Berries and a Body

Christmas Cookies and Criminals

Grapes, Ganache & Guilt

DUNE HOUSE COZY MYSTERIES

Seaside Secrets

Boats and Bad Guys

Treasured History

Hidden Hideaways

Dodgy Dealings

Suspects and Surprises

Ruffled Feathers

A Fishy Discovery

Danger in the Depths

Celebrities and Chaos

Pups, Pilots and Peril

Tides, Trails and Trouble

WAGGING TAIL COZY MYSTERIES

SAGE GARDENS COZY MYSTERIES

Sage Gardens Cozy Mystery Series Box Set Volume 1
(Books 1 - 4)

Birthdays Can Be Deadly

Money Can Be Deadly

Trust Can Be Deadly

Ties Can Be Deadly

Rocks Can Be Deadly

Jewelry Can Be Deadly

Numbers Can Be Deadly

Memories Can Be Deadly

Paintings Can Be Deadly

Snow Can Be Deadly

Tea Can Be Deadly

Greed Can Be Deadly

Clutter Can Be Deadly

NUTS ABOUT NUTS COZY MYSTERIES

A Tough Case to Crack

A Seed of Doubt

Roasted Peanuts and Peril

Chestnuts, Camping and Culprits

DONUT TRUCK COZY MYSTERIES

Deadly Deals and Donuts

Fatal Festive Donuts

Bunny Donuts and a Body

Strawberry Donuts and Scandal

Frosted Donuts and Fatal Falls

BEKKI THE BEAUTICIAN COZY MYSTERIES

Hairspray and Homicide

A Dyed Blonde and a Dead Body

Mascara and Murder

Pageant and Poison

Conditioner and a Corpse

Mistletoe, Makeup and Murder

Hairpin, Hair Dryer and Homicide

Blush, a Bride and a Body

Shampoo and a Stiff

Cosmetics, a Cruise and a Killer

Lipstick, a Long Iron and Lifeless

Camping, Concealer and Criminals

Treated and Dyed

A Wrinkle-Free Murder

A MACARON PATISSERIE COZY MYSTERY SERIES

Sifting for Suspects

Recipes and Revenge

Mansions, Macarons and Murder

HEAVENLY HIGHLAND INN COZY MYSTERIES

Murdering the Roses

Dead in the Daisies

Killing the Carnations

Drowning the Daffodils

Suffocating the Sunflowers

Books, Bullets and Blooms

A Deadly Serious Gardening Contest

A Bridal Bouquet and a Body

Digging for Dirt

WENDY THE WEDDING PLANNER COZY MYSTERIES

ABOUT THE AUTHOR

Cindy Bell is a USA Today and Wall Street Journal Bestselling Author. She is the author of the Little Leaf Creek, Wagging Tail, Donut Truck, Dune House, Sage Gardens, Chocolate Centered, Macaron Patisserie, Nuts about Nuts, Bekki the Beautician, Heavenly Highland Inn and Wendy the Wedding Planner cozy mystery series.

Cindy has always loved reading, but it is only recently that she has discovered her passion for writing romantic cozy mysteries. She loves walking along the beach thinking of the next adventure her characters can embark on.

You can sign up for her newsletter so you are notified of her latest releases at http://www.cindybellbooks.com.